MW01126070

Acknowledgements

First, as always, the highest praise and utmost gratitude to The Most High God, without whom nothing is possible. Thank you for continually blessing me on all of my endeavors in every area of my life.

If God is first, then my guardian angels must be second. Thank you to my sweet, handsome husband who continues to watch over me and our babies daily in everything we do. I miss you every single day, but I always remember that you're still with me, always by my side. May you live on through me and our beautiful children. To my brother and sister, James and Daniell Alexander, thank you as well for not only watching over me and mine, but all of us. Your babies look more and more like you with each passing day. To some of the most important men in my life: my brother Cedric, my father William, my father-in-law John, my grandfather George, and my grandfather-in-law Jessie... all I can ask is that y'all behave up there!

Special words of appreciation are in order for my team: my best friend, Danielle Holley, and my co-workers, Amy Tassin and Shonna Plant, whom the main character is named after and whose beauty is just as amazing. Thank you ladies for test reading the first draft and providing constructive criticism. Thank you to L'Vetrious Davis as well for just being there throughout the process and always challenging me to be my best self. Thank you to Winfred "Alex" Lee for encouraging me on an almost daily basis. For each of you the words "thank you" will never be enough. Also, thank you and innumerable blessings for Mr. Willie LeBlanc for all of the numerous services you have rendered during this process. From editing and formatting all the way down to advising me on the process. You are completely invaluable.

To my babies, Aniya and Master, you are the reasons I work long hours and cut my sleep short. Never ever forget that Momma loves you with everything in her, and just as Daddy did, he always will.

To my fans and loyal readers, I would be nothing without you. Thank you from the bottom of my heart! You guys rock!

Finally, to my characters, the little voices in my head that keep my pen going... As long as you keep telling me your stories, I'll keep writing them for the world to read.

To Aniya and Master
My Earthly Angels

Prologue

I plopped down on the plush white sofa with my bowl of grapes and threw my freshly pedicured feet up on the glass top of the coffee table. Grabbing the remote, I began flipping through the channels flashing on the projector screen.

"You missed a spot," I told Maurice as he was packing up his equipment without taking my eyes off of the television guide. I had two thousand channels and there was never anything worth watching on TV.

"Really?" he raised an eyebrow at me. "Where?"

"On the front of the sofa, three inches to the left of and two inches below my left leg." Maurice bent low, discovered the spot, and then looked up at me impressed.

"I apologize, ma'am."

"No apologies necessary. Just be sure to take especial care the next time. I think you'll find I'm not your average customer," I warned him.

"I think you'll find I'm not your average specialized custodian either, ma'am." I locked eyes with the elderly gentleman momentarily. He did not blink and did not look away. Neither did I. The silence said more than any words could have spoken. "If you'll excuse me, ma'am, I'll take care of that myself," he said as he nodded toward my legs which were obviously in the way.

2 -Slim Thick

I moved to the opposite end of the sofa, and Maurice bent down with some type of specialized spray and wiped the blood spatter off of the sofa with one swipe.

"With Luchesi out of the business," I spoke of his deceased competitor, "I'll be a more regular customer now, Maurice. But don't confuse it. I know people. And the people I know, know people as well. I have other options should your services prove to be less than sufficient and efficient." I looked him squarely in the eyes. "Do we have an understanding, Maurice?"

"Yes, ma'am," he said as the last of his crew exited through my front door. "Believe me, ma'am. We value your business, and you'll find us to be top of the line for your custodial and body removal needs."

"Good," I smiled as I rose. "Here is your fee I owe you for your services today. I'll be speaking with you."

"Yes, ma'am," he said as he tipped his bowler hat, picked up his briefcase, and followed his employees out. Deed done. Now I was free to watch the two episodes of Family Feud I had recorded because I knew I'd be preoccupied when they aired. Somehow I could always sense when someone was about to die. It was a gift- a blessing and a curse. And of course I would be able to sense when someone was about to die at my own hands.

I closed the French-style mahogany double doors by their Lalique handles and then plopped back down on the sofa. My mind began to wander a bit as I retrieved the recorded episodes on the DVR. The fact that this shit was going to have to stop eventually had never run across my mind, but for some reason, it did at that moment. My body count was already ridiculous, and I was suddenly considered the wear and tear the cleaning chemicals would have on my Italian marble floors.

Life had not always been like this for me. At one point in my life, I never could have seen myself slicing the throats of low-lives and having them cleaned up off of my living room floor by a professional black market body removal service. It's funny how life can take you down some of the most twisted roads you could have ever imagined. But one thing life has taught me: these mother fuckers ain't no friend to you, even the ones who are kin to you.

Chapter 1

I jumped up out of my sleep in a panic. It was eleven forty-five at night and my body was programmed to wake up at ten-thirty every evening. I had been working the grave-yard shift seven days a week and this was my first off day in six months at the Nike Warehouse. Rolling over, I snuggled beneath Curtis, my husband of seven years. He wrapped his arms around me, and I attempted to fall back asleep, but to no avail. After laying there for an hour, I finally decided to get up to avoid waking my husband.

I quietly busied myself in the kitchen making a sand-wich while a can of Campbell's Vegetable Soup heated up in the microwave. Curtis had to be at work at five-thirty at the Hershey plant, so I didn't want to wake him from the sleep I knew he needed for his twelve-hour shift. As I sat down on the living room sofa, I thought about the seven long years Curtis and I had been married and the demanding schedules we had been working. I couldn't figure out how we had made it work for so long, but I guess it's just like they say: Nothing is perfect, but love makes it worth it.

Curtis and I had lived a quiet life our entire marriage. We both were college graduates, but neither of us had found jobs utilizing our degrees in Memphis' strained job market. We didn't have any children- not because we didn't want any, but I believed it was because my stress level, lack of sleep, and poor eating habits had prevented me from conceiving. Whatever the biological reason, Curtis had been more than understanding, and he and I both believed that God would bless us with our own bundle of joy when the time was right.

I loved that man. I loved that man with everything in me- every breath, every bone, every drop of blood, every string in my heart. I had my head so far up that man's ass, I couldn't see down the street without him telling me to look. But it was mutual, and to me, that's what life and love was all about: loving someone who loved you back.

Curtis wasn't like other men from our hood. He was a thug-gone-good. He had been involved in all kinds of criminal activity when he was younger, but he said I changed him. He said I made him want to do better and I gave him a reason to. He had enrolled in college a year after I had; traded in his baggy jeans, white t-shirts, and Timbs and Forces for Ralph Lauren Polo shirts, button-downs, khakis, and loafers; and refocused his energy and attention to living the family life. I thanked God for him, his maturity, and his mindset every day. Lord knows I had seen too many of my friends being taken down through there by the men they loved.

Suddenly, there was a loud boom at our kitchen door and items that had been on our kitchen counter were sent flying across the floor. I jumped up as three masked men pointed a sawed-off and two handguns at my forehead.

"Bitch, where the fuck Curt at?" the one with the sawed-off yelled at me, but my husband was already coming down the hallway. Educated or not, I was still from the hood. I knew not to tell their asses shit. The taller of the two with the handguns turned and pointed his gun at Curtis.

"Where the money and shit at?" he yelled. I looked at Curtis and frowned. I knew my husband like the back of my hand. The look on his face told me that despite my ignorance,

6 -Slim Thick

he knew exactly what they were talking about and wasn't about to tell them shit. I saw the two black pistols in his hands and the look in his eyes as he stared into mine from down the hall. He blinked…just one second too long. The signal. I dropped to the floor.

Just a millisecond after the top of my head had cleared the barrel of the shot gun, Mr. Sawed-Off was lying on the floor next to me, the nerves in his body still jumping as he bled out from the hole in the side of his head. I screamed at the sight as Curtis continued firing shots at the two remaining intruders who were dodging his bullets. The one who was closest to me snatched me up off of the floor and put the barrel of his pistol to my temple. Time stood still as I stared pleading into my husband's eyes.

"Motherfucker, I'mma ask you one more time where the mother fucking guns, money, and drugs at before I blow this bitch's noodles all over this mother fucking wall."

"I love that woman more than I love myself and she knows it," he said to them as he stared back at me.

"Love…" I whispered, and he raised his gun at the man standing closest to him and was shot square between his eyes.

I don't remember hearing myself scream as I watched the life leave out of my husband's eyes. I remember the momentary chaos between the two goons…and then I blacked out.

~ * ~ * ~ * ~

When I finally came to, I found myself lying on a naked mattress on the concrete floor of an abandoned warehouse with my mouth covered and ankles and wrists bound by zebra print duct tape. I quickly surveyed my surroundings without moving my head to avoid giving any indication that I was conscious. I was in an empty room with concrete floors, ceilings, and walls, but I could see that outside of the room morning sunlight was pouring in through high windows, dozens of stacks of wooden pallets were piled almost to the ceiling and there was an area separated by a chain-link fence with tables inside of it. Male voices unmuffled by their masks echoed in the emptiness as they discussed my lack of consciousness with impatience.

Suddenly, one peeked his head around the corner of the door and I hurriedly closed my eyes again. This went on for hours as they discussed what they could and would do to get information out of me. I busied myself attempting to wet the duct tape with my lips and tongue until I could unpeel it from my mouth.

By the time the sunlight shining into the windows began showed signs that it was mid-afternoon, the two watchmen had grown impatient and I knew I was in trouble. The shooter who had killed my husband came into the room and marched straight over to me. Snatching me up by my hair, he slapped the shit out of me. With that first lick, I tasted blood and I already knew what was about to happen. He ripped the tape from my mouth with one solid swipe and I spit out a mouthful of the blood and saliva mixture.

"Bitch, I'mma give you one chance to tell me where the fuck Curt got the money and shit stashed. Don't feed me no bullshit about you don't know where the shit at cuz I know you know. Tell me where the shit at and you can go home and bury your nigga and piece your life back together. The longer you stand here and bullshit me, the longer you gone be here. You take too long, you ain't gone leave this motherfucker alive. You feel me?"

"I don't know about any drugs," I told him. "And that's the honest to God truth."

From that moment on, they didn't ask me anything else. Every hour they would come into the room and proceed to beat the shit out of me as if it was going to suddenly jog my memory. The problem is that not only did I not know where the "money and shit" were, I had absolutely no knowledge of the criminal ass shit my husband had been doing behind my back.

This went on for seven straight days. Between the beatings, I would watch the sunlight change in the windows outside of the room to count the passing days. Twice a day they fed me half-done ramen noodles on a plate so they wouldn't have to untie my wrists. Twice I tried to scream out for help, but my nose was met by the toe of an over-worn Nike Air Force One. It didn't matter. My nose had been broken since the first day I got there and I doubted it would ever look the same again. My eyes were both blacked and had started to heal. My lips felt like they were permanently swollen. I had almost become immune to pain, having been hit in the same spots over and over again. I had knots on top of knots, bruised bruises, wounded wounds.

Over the course of the week, I had heard them call each

other by the names "Lil Don" and "Glenn". The first few nights they had taken turns spending the night inside of the warehouse to guard me and make sure I didn't break out and get away. But Glenn had already been kicked in the balls twice for thinking he was going to creep up on me in the middle of the night and dip into my cookie jar. I was defenseless when it came to them attacking me, but in the near blackness of the night warehouse, he was the one with the disadvantage. I couldn't move my hands, but he couldn't see my feet coming either.

I had also pieced together that Curtis had been living his secret life while I was at work. Because I worked overnight, I was unaware that my husband had been spending the majority of his nights conducting very large drug transactions. Apparently he had started out running money for different drug dealers until he had come up with enough money to buy his way into the business. I knew my husband: Curtis was a math and business genius. So it was of no surprise to me to find out that from that point, Curtis' drug business had grown steadily. When Glenn, Lil Don, and their deceased accomplice, Rakeem, had come bursting into my kitchen door, they had expected to find at least several kilos of Coke and pounds of weed stashed in our house. That said enough to me.

None of that bothered me as much as I once thought it would. I was beyond disappointed that my husband would hide something so important and potentially deadly from me, but I also knew my husband's heart. He was doing what he felt he had to do to provide for the two of us, and if I knew him like I thought I did, I knew that he was trying to save up money so that I could stop working and go back to school again and to build a nest egg for the baby he and I were hoping to one day birth. I had noticed the pained look on his face every time I got dressed for work, but even worse was the look when he realized my monthly had returned yet again every month on schedule. We had had many conversations about my long hours and absence of days off, and we both wondered if the stress from my job was the culprit for my lack of conception.

On the eighth day the two men stormed into the warehouse at the moment the sun was high enough to peek into the windows. The look on Lil Don's face told me something had changed.

"Get up, bitch!" he yelled as he entered the room. I had heard the familiar sound of the heavy metal door slamming as they entered the building, but I could barely keep my eyes open. Already paranoid because of my circumstances, I hadn't gotten much sleep at all during the night due to the tears of loneliness and loss as thoughts and memories of my husband flooded my mind and pierced my heart.

"My husband! They took my husband from me! Oh, Curtis, baby!" I had cried out in the middle of the night. But there were no ears nearby to hear.

Glenn snatched me up by my hair, drug me out of the room, and tossed me into a metal folding chair that was set up between two stacks of pallets on the warehouse floor. Until this point, I had only been beaten and starved. Lil Don picked up a hot curling iron and approached me with it. I forced myself up, trying to get away from him, but tripped over my own two bound feet and fell flat on my face. The curling iron sizzled on the back of my sweaty neck, and I screamed in agony.

Over and over again, I was burned with the curling iron, sliced with a large butcher knife, and shocked with a corner store quality taser. I just knew I would bleed out or lose consciousness from the pain as they continued to torture me over the next week, but somehow, I managed to maintain.

One day in the middle of the second week, Lil Don came through the door complaining to Glenn that his girlfriend was becoming suspicious about him being away from home, had accused him of cheating on her, and had refused to have sex with him the night before. Glenn attempted to reassure Lil Don that all of his time away from his girlfriend would soon pay off when they got the information they were seeking out of me, but Lil Don warned Glenn that he had better hope so because his lies were no longer keeping his girlfriend at bay.

Two days later, I looked at them both as they rounded the corner into my little empty-ass cold-ass room. I had never really looked at them, examined them. Glenn looked like he liked bright skinned prissy bitches with long Peruvian (that was probably actually Yaki) and eye lash extensions big enough to pick them up and fly away with them if they batted them too hard. The bitches that pretended to be Red Lobster and Dom Perignon material, but really weren't worth more than a pack of Ramen noodles and a bottle of store brand purified water- not even the Ozarka natural spring water.

Lil Don looked like he liked nothing but hood rats. Hoes that pretended to be wifey material but really would spread their legs for the whole hood. Ugly bitches that transform like Optimus Prime after an hour long session in the mirror talking to Mac and Lancome. Hell, if I had to guess, I was willing to bet good money that his girlfriend was one of those bitches that even make-up couldn't help. One of the ones that still wore black lipstick and black lip liner and was shaped like Spongebob Squarepants. One of those bitches that her boyfriend knows she's ugly, but doesn't have the heart to be honest with her, so he always says shit like, "Beauty is only skin deep" and "she has a heart of gold" and "looks ain't everything." Looks may not be everything, but, damn, I at least need to be able to hold my food down while you're on top of me. But, hey, that shit was none of my business.

I fought back my laughter as that thought ran through my head as Lil Don was complaining again about the lack of sexual activity at his place of residence as they entered the room. He caught the last bit of it that I was attempting to swallow.

"Bitch, what the fuck you laughing at?" He snatched me up by my hair. "You think this shit is funny? I'mma fuck you up!"

My thoughts had turned completely cynical and sarcastic at this point. I guess it was my own way of keeping myself sane. I wonder what else he could possibly do to me. Rape me? I was sure Glenn had warned him about my almost perfect aim with my feet.

"A whole nother night," he said as he dragged me with my knotted, matted curls between his fingers. "A whole nother night with no pussy 'cause your weak ass still ain't told me where your nigga's weed and shit at. Bitch, I'm gone beat you to death. You know that, right? You gone die trying to protect this dead ass nigga that can't do shit to help you."

He threw me into the same chair he had tossed my small

beaten and bloody frame into before. I had barely landed in the seat of the chair when he slapped me back out of it. It felt like he slapped an entirely different state of mind into me at that moment. I tasted my own blood in my mouth again and something just snapped in my head. When he lifted me back into the chair, I just kept my eyes closed and tried to zone out with thoughts of my deceased husband as Lil Don beat me relentlessly until he dislocated his knuckles in his right hand.

"Aaaggghhhh!" he screamed out. "You stupid bitch!" He kicked me in my stomach so hard that the chair fell backwards with me in it. "If Glenn wasn't here, I'd fuck you in every hole you got, put a bullet in your skull, and dump your ass in the river!"

I just laid there. I didn't respond and didn't even bother trying to open my eyes. They were swollen shut...again.

"Don, mane, c'mon, man," Glenn said. "Let's just go ahead and leave for the day. You've already fucked your hand up. Let's just gone and go, man."

"Man, put the bitch in the room before I kill her funky ass," he told him, and with that, Glenn gathered me up in the most gentle way he had handled me the entire time and sat me back down on the flat mattress in the cold little room and the two of them left.

I decided right then and there that I couldn't and wouldn't take it any longer. I was going to figure out a way to escape that night, and I didn't care if I died trying. I hadn't tried to open the door of the room in over a week because every time I shimmied over to the door and attempted to open it, it was always locked. I decided to give it another try.

I allowed myself to doze off for a few hours, deciding that my best chance to get away would come after night fall. When it finally came, the swelling in my eyes had gone down enough that I could partially see through them, so I felt my way to the door and tried the knob. I gasped as it opened. It was still daylight outside and the sun was still shining through the high warehouse windows. I frantically looked around, spotted the exit door, and ran to it. It was locked.

As I stood there in a panic, I looked around for anything that could pry or wedge the door open, but there was nothing. I was ready to go. I had already been in that hell hole for two weeks, been tortured, starved, and treated like an animal, and beaten into an unrecognizable pulp. I couldn't stand the thought of being held there one moment longer, and yet, it was a fact I was forced to accept.

Chapter 2

Instead of fleeing and running for my life, I was forced to construct a plan to escape when my two captors returned. I gathered all of the items they had used to torture me and piled them behind the door. Then I sat down and sorted through them. But when I thought about it, I actually didn't need any of them. What I needed was a sturdy 2 x 4 or pipe that I could knock their asses out with.

I searched through the warehouse for loose wooden planks until I finally found one that was not dry-rotted or termite-infested. On my way back to the doorway, I walked through the warehouse a bit and discovered a ridiculous amount of cocaine, marijuana, and what must have been crystal meth piled on top of tables in a corner. I was no drug dealer, but these niggas had me fucked up. I decided right then that when I was able to escape, I'd load whatever I could into whatever vehicle the two thugs were driving and make a clean get away with their stash.

I brought the plank back to the doorway and sat there waiting for the sunlight to peek into the warehouse through the windows. The moment it did, I stood up, grabbed my plank, and waited. I stood there in position for twenty minutes before I heard the key turn in the lock. Glenn strutted in first and I let him pass. Lil Don always came in second because Glenn had the key. Lil Don, however, always had the gun. As soon as Lil Don cleared the doorway, I swung the plank as hard as I could and he landed on his face at my feet.

As Glenn spun around to see what the commotion was,

16 –Slim Thick

I hurriedly grabbed the .38 revolver from Lil Don's hip and aimed it straight at Glenn's nose. He took one step toward me and I cocked the gun.

"Don't come any closer to me or I'll kill you, bitch," I told him. My hands were visibly shaking from the adrenaline, but I meant every word I said.

"Bitch?" he chuckled. "Hoe, I'm gone beat your ass and then fuck the shit outta you and then dump your deformed ass in the river for the catfish to eat."

"Over my dead body, bitch boy," I told him and then shot him in the leg as he lunged at me. His screams echoed in the open warehouse as he hit the concrete floor next to his accomplice. "Shut the fuck up, bitch!" I said as I kicked him in his mouth just as he had done me. I was barefoot, though, and the kick hurt me just as much as it hurt him.

"Bitch, I'm gone kill you!" Glenn threatened again. I just laughed. "D, wake up! Lil Don! Wake up, fool!"

Lil Don stirred slightly but remained unconscious. I could have left. I should have left. But something in me just wouldn't let me leave. They had tortured me for two weeks straight. As much as my mom had kept me in church and as many times as I had heard "Vengeance is mine, said the Lord," I still could not allow them to get off the easily. I looked at Glenn laying there crying over his busted knee cap and then at Lil Don who was drooling onto the concrete. I looked at the open door… and closed it.

Glenn frowned at me and then watched as I picked up the

roll of zebra print duct tape. He tried to get up as I taped up Lil Don, but I pointed the gun at him again.

"Try to pull any bullshit, and I'll blow your other knee clean smooth off," I warned him. This time there was no doubt in his eyes. He knew I'd shoot him. He sat back down as I taped Lil Don's mouth closed and then began shaking his head as I came closer to him with the roll.

"You're not about to tape me up. You got me fucked up," he told me. I laughed in his face. What was he going to do to stop me? I picked up the taser and before he could even move a full inch, I had stuck the taser between his legs and pressed the button. I wasn't going to keep playing with them, especially this would-be rapist lying on the floor with one good knee cap.

When I let the button go, I grabbed both of his wrists and quickly taped them behind his back. There really wasn't much need to tape his ankles, but I did so anyway. When the shock wore off, he began screaming at the top of his lungs.

"You can scream all you want to," I laughed. "Nobody can hear you. Nobody will come. Nobody will hear you but me and your little buddy here. And since I don't want to hear the shit, how about I just shut you up?" I said as I tore a strip of tape and slapped it over his lips.

I let him lie there and watch me load package after package of marijuana and cocaine into his Chevy Tahoe after I snatched his set of keys from him. I knew that crystal meth shit had a high value as well, but I just wasn't about to take that chance with it because I knew it carried high jail time. I made sure to place the packages in the back of the SUV neatly and tightly so that I could fit it all inside. As the packages dwindled down, they revealed a cabinet that had been hidden behind them. I sat the package of weed that I was holding down on the floor and opened the cabinet door.

"Oh shit," I whispered. "Holy shit!" Both of my hands covered my mouth in shock. There were stacks and stacks of packages inside of the cabinet equal in size to the pounds of weed and kilos of Coke...but it was all one hundred, fifty, and twenty dollar bills.

I finished walking the drugs out to the truck as Glenn watched, but when I started carrying out the money, he started screaming again from deep down in his throat and flopping around like a fish out of water. I just laughed and then acted like I didn't even hear him. None of that was going to make a damned difference. If anything, it was only making his situation worse because he was getting on my last damned nerve.

When I had loaded everything I was going to take, I looked back at him and just couldn't resist. Glenn's screaming had caused Lil Don to regain consciousness, and now he was screaming as well. When he had open his eyes, he realized he was hog-tied and his mouth was taped shut, but it was Glenn's bloody knee that sent him into a panic.

"You were going to rape me," I looked Glenn in his eyes and told him. "You tried to sneak up on me and rape me while your friend here was gone at night. Not only are you a thief and a murderer, but you're a molester too. You're the scum of the fucking earth," I said and then jammed the taser between his legs again. Lil Don screamed with him in horror.

"And you," I said as I turned to Lil Don. "You killed my husband and then beat me because your bitch wouldn't fuck you because you'd been here with me all night. Then you wanted to rape me too because you couldn't get no pussy at home!" I shocked him even longer than I had shocked Glenn and watched as he shook involuntarily. "Bitch!" I yelled as I kicked him in the face afterwards and watched his nose drip crimson blood. I plugged up the curling iron and watched it grow hotter and hotter as I twirled the butcher knife between two fingers.

"You bitches don't even deserve the time I'm about to put into making the last few hours of your lives and living hell, but shooting you and getting it over with would be letting you off too easy," I taunted them.

"You beat me and beat me, trying to get information from me that I never had. How does it feel to know you did all of that, got no information, and are about to die?" I looked Lil Don squarely in his eyes. "How does it feel?!" I screamed at him. "How does it feel to see death walking toward you one step at a time and not be able to do anything at all to stop him? To be bound and tied up when your life and your survival are resting in your own hands? NO one here is going to save you. You realize that, don't you? You think this nigga is your friend?" I asked as I kicked Glenn in his nose with the heel of my foot and listened to him scream in agony.

"Do you?" I yelled at Lil Don with my foot still resting on Glenn's face. "Do you think for one second that he's risk his own life to save yours? He's your homie, ain't he? You think he'll take a bullet for you?" I cocked the gun. "Let's see if he'll volunteer to die if it means you'll live." I pointed the gun at Glenn's head.

"You gone take this bullet for him? Take one for the team?" Glenn looked back and forth between me and Lil Don. I bent down and put the hole to his dome. "Y'all ruthless, right? Come on, Loc. At least you gone die with honor." Glenn shook his head with tears pouring from his eyes. "It ain't no ride or die, Cuz. If you riding, you dying. So what's up?" He shook his head profusely, and I laughed in his face.

"You see this shit?" I turned to Lil Don. "Your homie just gone let you die. He ain't even gone take one for the team. Maybe he's worth more than you are. You gone go ahead and take this bullet to save his life?" He squinted his eyes at me. "Are you daring me? Is that a challenge? You think I won't shoot your bitch ass too? You take me for a joke, huh? Well, let me show you I'm not playing." I pressed the barrel flat against the crotch of his jeans and pulled the trigger.

I've never seen a human flop around so uncontrollably as a man who had just lost his penis. I made Glenn watch as Lil Don bled out, lost consciousness, and then stopped breathing. When it was obvious that Lil Don was dead, I looked back at Glenn. He was terrified. It was written all over his face; it was obvious in his eyes.

"Now what should I do with you?" I said as I twirled the butcher knife. "Hmmm," I thought out loud. "Maybe I should collect your fingers one by one," I said and watched his facial expression. "Or maybe I should slice off your ears since you hated to hear my screams and cries for help. Well! One thing for sure! I need to repossess this bullet from your knee," I said and slid the tip of the blade of the knife deep into his wound. His deep, throaty screams were like music to my ears; his sweat and tears were like a beautiful painting of the rarest rose.

He huffed and puffed as I removed the knife. My curiosity was piqued. I could torture him and get away with it. I could explore every part of the human body I had ever been curious about. No, I thought to myself. You don't have time to do that kind of shit. They may change your whole outlook on life, but don't let them take your humanity.

And yet, there was another voice deep within who no longer gave two fucks about a heart or my humanity. Fuck him, that voice said. Let's see what that ball looks like inside a nigga's nuts.

I laid the knife on top of the sizzling curling iron. Glenn, who was still writhing in pain, didn't even notice. I walked over to him, unbuckled his pants, and pulled them down to his ankles. He looked at me confused, not knowing what to expect. I gently ran my hands up his stomach and chest seductively.

"You wanted to fuck me, didn't you?" I whispered. "You want this pussy? I bet you got a big dick too." I ran my fingertips over the lump in his boxers. The voice in my head was laughing hysterically at his misfortune. Big where? His left nut was probably bigger than his dick. His demeanor calmed a bit, though I could tell he was still in pain. I pulled down his boxers.

I needed some gloves. I'm surprised I didn't throw up. This nigga had to be experiencing the worst herpes outbreak

I had ever seen, even in comparison to Facebook and rotten. com.

"So this is what you were going to fuck me with?" I frowned at him. "So you were going to fuck me with this little bitty ass sick dick?" I watched the fear growing in his eyes. "Bet, bitch!"

I got up and went back to the cabinet I had discovered behind the piles of drugs and found the roll of seran wrap. I wrapped my hands up tight and returned walked at a brisk pace. I swiped the hot knife and secured a firm grip on Glenn's balls, all in one swift smooth motion.

"I'm finna neuter your ass. On the count of four, I'm going to slice off your nuts and watch you bleed out." Glenn squirmed, trying to get away, but he was only hurting himself in my grip. "Relax, relax," I whispered to him. He screamed. "Sssshhh, relax."

I counted to two and sliced his balls smooth off and enjoyed the shriek he let out. I watched as blood poured and formed a pool around him. Weak ass trick, I thought to myself. And when he took his last breath, I smashed the breaker box with the 2x4 and locked their roguish asses up to rot in the same prison they had provided for me.

Chapter 3

The police, my family, and my friends had all been looking for me. The FBI had gotten involved and a reward for my return or any information on my whereabouts had been offered. My mother and father in law had already handled my husband's affairs. From what I was told, the funeral was nice. My husband looked like his normal handsome self and he was buried next to his grandparents in a double dip plot. They thought I was dead. So they had been prepared to bury me with my husband.

I didn't say much to anybody. I spent two days in a rundown motel to get myself some sleep, and it took every-thing in me not to shower or bathe. I knew my mother had to be at work at seven in the morning, so at six-thirty I laid my ass on her porch in the same pajamas I had been wearing since I had crawled from beneath my husband to warm up a bowl of soup. She came out the door headed to work and screamed when she saw me lying in front of her front door a beaten, bloody, swollen mess.

I had walked the four miles from the motel to my mom's house, taking all back streets to avoid being spotted. I was sweaty, and I was sure I must have smelled foul, though I could no longer smell myself.

I gave my statement to the police and turned down their offers of protection in case the guys decided to come back and kidnap me again, siting my desire to try to return to as much of a normal life as possible. There was nothing normal about how my life was turning out or where it was headed and I knew it. I had already led what I thought was a normal life, and look where it had gotten me. There was no more staying quiet and playing by the rules for me. Life as I knew it had come to an end the day my husband took his last breath.

Over the next few days, I moved the Tahoe around from motel to motel and even rented rooms at some of them to divert suspicion. Each night, I would load two packages of money and two packages of drugs into my own car and take them home. I stored them in the second bedroom and made sure to keep the blinds and curtains closed at all times.

During the day, I busied myself pulling credit card, telephone, and banking records. I looked into every piece of my husband's life to find everything I could. The insurance company had already contacted me to collect the remainder of Curtis' life insurance policy, so I knew that even more money was coming soon. The entire time I felt that there was something that I was missing, something that I was overlooking.

I had spent every night- whether at home or in a motel room- balled up in a fetal position crying my eyes out because of the unescapable memory of my husband dropping dead to the floor in the middle of the same hallway I walked through every day. I'd hear him drop his keys on the living room table in the middle of the night. I'd smell his scent in the bedroom after being gone all day. I'd hear his voice whispering his 'I love you's' in my ear and then laughing uncontrollably at one of our multiple inside jokes.

The daydreams at noon were accompanied by the nightmares at midnight, so my every moment was a living hell. I had no one and nothing and neither did I want anything. Nothing could bring my husband back to me, and yet he was the only thing that mattered and the only thing I desired. I had numbed my senses to survive in the warehouse, but now I was struggling not to allow all of my feelings to come bursting out at once. I was struggling to accept my new reality, and struggling even more not to slip into insanity.

Three weeks of sobbing into my pillow and screaming into the darkness later, I thought I was losing my mind when a letter came to the house addressed to me from a bank in Chicago. I hadn't been to Chicago since I was fourteen, and I had no idea Curtis had been there. But the letter told me otherwise. Not only did Curtis have an account at this bank, but it was so sizable that they were asking that I go to Chicago to sign paperwork to collect. And so I did.

I told nobody anything. I had already moved all of the money and drugs into my house and disposed of the Tahoe. I had no other real obligation. I pack a bag, rented a car, and drove from Memphis to Chicago without even calling my mother. When I made it into the city, I got a room at the Four Seasons, had dinner at Pizzeria Uno, had a Sex on the Beach at the hotel bar, and took my ass to sleep in the plush ass bed in my suite. I hadn't slept that well even before Curtis died, but I knew I owed myself only the best.

Seven hundred forty-eight thousand, one hundred three dollars. Almost three quarters of a million dollars. I was the only beneficiary of the account of which I previously had no knowledge. While at the International Bank of Chicago, I requested all of Curtis' bank records so that I could research his transactions when I made it home.

26 - Slim Thick

When I left the bank, I went shopping. I had brought twenty-five thousand in cash with me with every intention of blowing it on the latest fashions. I loaded my trunk with bags from Gucci, Coach, Michael Kors, Nordstrom, BVLGARI, True Religion, Armani, Aldo, and White House Black Market. I bought things I had never seen before at prices I had never been able to afford. It was in Chicago that I purchased my very first pair of Christian Louboutin heels. Red bottoms. But it was also in Chicago that I found and fell in love with Jimmy Choos. I bought seven pairs of them in one mall and found myself addicted. It was like there was no design that was not flawless if it had the Jimmy Choo name on it. I was hooked. After my shopping spree, I jumped right back onto the interstate and drove the seven hours back to Memphis with my check in one of my new Michael Kors bags.

Chapter 4

Seven hundred forty-eight thousand dollars. Seven hundred forty-eight thousand dollars. My husband had nearly a million dollars in a Chicago savings account, and I had been working twelve hour shifts seven days a week and living in this little bitty ass piece of shit ass rental house in the hood. I had told myself it could've been worse. He could've had a side chick and two outside kids, but none of that was the case. He was as committed to me as he could possibly be. And yet, it seemed he was still living a double life.

Curtis had hidden every aspect of his second life from me. But when I returned home from Chicago, everything unraveled for me. Three nights after I came back from Chicago, I was up all night, unable to sleep. Dreams of Curtis had been waking me up throughout the night ever since I made it back to my own bed. He was pestering me, trying to tell me something, but I couldn't figure out what it was. I finally gave up trying to sleep and went into the living room and laid across the couch. I let the TV play that infomercial Curtis liked. You know, the one for the Time Life collection of all of the 70's, 80's, and 90's R&B love songs. I hate infomercials because they always advertise for the low low price of some outrageous amount of money from some bullshit. But something about it comforted me at that moment, so I didn't bother changing the channel.

The folder of Curtis' bank records from his account in Chicago had been lying on the coffee table since I dropped it there on my way to the bedroom with both arms full of shopping bags. I picked it up and decided to go ahead and look through it. I grabbed the legal pad I had been taking notes on and my little stacks of Post-It Notes and flags, and said a little prayer like I always did that I wouldn't find anything that would break my heart or ruin my memory of who I believed my husband to be.

It was quite the contrary. Obviously Curtis knew that I would have access to his records because he left me as beneficiary of the account. It became evident that Curtis was relying on me pulling those records to inform me of everything else he had been doing. This account was how Curtis had been managing his drug money.

There were frequent deposits and withdrawals of large sums of money, amounts large enough to equal about three or more months of Curtis' paychecks being moved around as frequently as twice in one week. There would be a withdrawal of up to ten thousand dollars followed by several deposits of fifteen and twenty thousand dollars. The account had been open for five years, and this was the nature of the transactions for the first two years.

Early in the third fiscal year, Curtis' account balance of nearly two million dollars suddenly dropped by half. There was a withdrawal for thirty thousand dollars that was paid to Shelby County, Tennessee. I used the transaction number on the account record to find Curtis' payment on the website. He had bought five acres of land in unincorporated Shelby County. Five acres of land. I just knew the nigga must've been starting a farm.

The next month, there was a two hundred fifty thousand dollar transfer to First Financial Bank. Then the same transfer each month the following seven months. As baffled as I was about the transfers, there were other items on the records that I knew I had to look into as well. Cell phone payments for a number I didn't recognize. Several payments for safety deposit boxes at different banks in Memphis, Chicago, St. Louis, Atlanta, Las Vegas, Dallas, Kansas City, Los Angeles, Seattle, and Reno. One particular safety deposit box in New York had been upgraded in size four times. Twenty acres of land had been purchased in Arizona during the fourth year, and then another million dollars transferred to a bank there. Large jewelry purchases from various jewelers. There were two car purchases from "Exotic Foreign Customs" in Phoenix that totaled almost a quarter of a million dollars.

I may have been blind all of those years and I may have been innocent, but I was far from stupid. Just by looking at the bank records, I knew there were at least two very large houses in the country with my name on the deeds. I also knew that if Curtis felt comfortable enough to make these sizes of purchases with this account and leave the balance at less than a million, there had to have been other accounts out there equal or larger in size.

The next day, I went down to First Financial Bank. It seemed they had been waiting for my arrival.

"Mrs. Taylor, right this way, please," a middle-aged, handsome man wearing a suit and an impeccable fade greeted me. He led me to his office- not a cubicle- and closed the door behind us. "Please, have a seat," he ushered me to the leather chairs facing his desk. I placed my purse in the chair next to mine and sat down, crossing my legs in my red skirt. "Mrs. Taylor, I'm Bradford Cummings. I'm over the loan department here at First Financial, but I'm also your husband's financial advisor. Much more importantly, Curtis was a very dear friend of mine."

"So then you'll be able to tell me what's going on," I raised an eyebrow at him.

"Mrs. Taylor, in my place of business I can only disclose a limited amount of information. Your husband did in fact leave us specific instructions for your arrival here after his death. He has incredible faith in your abilities to interpret minimal information, but everything you need to obtain all of your assets is in your husband's safety deposit box here in our vault," he explained.

"So my husband knew he was going to die and prepared everything for me?"

"Your husband was prepared to die and knew what you would need in that event," he clarified. "This is the key to your husband's box. I'll escort you to the vault."

Inside of the vault, Mr. Cummings had set up a table for me to lie out and sort through the contents of Curtis' box. He unlocked Curtis' box, slid it out of the slot, and sat it down on the table in front of me.

"I'll be in my office if you need me. Please stop by before you leave," he said and nodded as he left the room.

For a second, I just sat there looking at the box. There was no telling what I was going to find inside. I told myself I should go ahead and get it over with because though I knew nothing of my husband's secondary lifestyle, I knew my husband, his love for me, and his character very well.

When I opened the box, the first thing that caught my eye was an envelope on top of all of the other contents. "Shonna" was written in Curtis' neat handwriting. Tears welled in my eyes, but I fought them back. Whatever was written in the letter inside of the envelope, I decided, was going to have to wait until I got home. There was a series of yellow envelopes, most of them labeled. There were five envelopes with ten thousand dollars inside each of them. There were several Tiffany & Co. boxes, the smallest of which I opened to find a beautiful set of wedding bands. I immediately slid the women's bands onto my hand, but then thought twice about it and put them back in the box. The other jewelry boxes contained necklaces, bracelets, chains, rings, and watches. I dropped all of the boxes and envelopes in my purse, closed the empty deposit box, and went back to Mr. Cummings' office.

"That was quick. Are you finished?" he asked.

"Yes," I nodded. "I'll sort through everything at home."

"Well, if you'll sign here," he said as he drew an X on a form, "I have the balance of Curtis' account here for you." He nodded at the black duffle bag in the chair where I had initially sat my purse. I checked the balance as I signed. Another eight hundred thousand. "Also, Mr. Taylor did advise us that the deed to the land and house he purchased through our bank is inside of one of those envelopes that was inside of his deposit box. I think you'll find it more than accommodating."

The insinuation dripped from his lips.

"I'm sorry," I said as I shook my head. "This is all a bit much."

"Shonna," he rose from his chair and stepped around his desk. "Curtis loved you very, very much. Everything he did- his method and his motive- was for you. I'm a bit out of line right now, but my best advice to you at this moment is to go home, pack up everything you just can't leave behind, and move into this house. When you move out of your old house, don't ever under any circumstances go back there. You aren't safe there, which is evident in what happened there."

"I understand," I nodded to him. "Thank you so much, Mr. Cummings."

"Brad. You can call me Brad," he corrected me. "And if you need me for anything, don't hesitate to call me." He handed me his personal card.

"Thanks, Brad."

"Here, I'll see you to your car," he said as he held the door open for me. He walked me to my car and opened my door for me. "Shonna," he said as I tossed the duffel bag on the passenger seat. I turned to face him. "I know by now you know this money isn't honest money. All money isn't good money, but this money is yours now. It's a chance for you to start your life over. Curtis did everything he could to protect you from his lifestyle. Just be careful. Be extra careful."

"I... I will, Brad. Thank you."

Slim Thick- 33

I drove off from that bank thinking, This nigga must be crazy. I had at least eight million in cash in my possession now. There was enough cocaine in my house to buy myself another mansion. There was enough weed to buy a couple of cars too. I was nothing but trouble at that moment, and I knew it.

When I got home, I put the jewelry in the duffel bag and tossed it into the room with the rest of the money and drugs. I took all of the envelopes and spread them across the coffee table. I picked out the "Shonna" envelope and sat it on the couch next to me. I didn't have time for Curtis' "dear Shonna" sentiments at that moment.

I started opening envelopes. The first one I opened held the deed, the keys, and a list of codes to the house in Arizona. The second one held the same for the house in Memphis. The third envelope held titles to a Porsche Cayenne, Audi R8, and Land Rover Range Rover. I had no clue where the cars were, but my little Chevy Malibu wasn't shit compared to these cars. Hell, neither was Curtis' Infiniti G35 he had been riding around in.

I kept opening envelopes. Money, money, money. There were keys to the deposit boxes I saw listed on the bank records. There was an envelope with three copies of Curtis' birth certificate. There was also an envelope with copies of both of our credit reports. Passports for both of us were in yet another envelope. Paperwork and codes were in three other envelopes- off shore accounts. Just how much work had my husband really been moving? I opened another envelope and gasped as tears filled my eyes. Three copies of my birth certificate.

Chapter 5

Curtis Taylor and I met in the ninth grade. We were best friends until the beginning of our senior year when one of our weekly study sessions turned into something much more. Curtis knew everything about me- from my birthday, favorite song and color, to my entire childhood history.

I was an orphan. My mother, whoever she was, was a fifteen-year-old girl who got caught up in a bad situation. She gave me up for adoption the day I was born, and I never heard from her again. When I was three, a nice couple came into the orphanage and picked me out like a puppy in the window, paid some money, signed some paperwork, and poof! I belonged to them. They never lied to me by telling me I was their biological child, but they always assured me and reminded me that they loved me just as if they had birthed me. I was the child that my adoptive mother had always wanted but could never have.

I was born Shoshonna Franklin. Shoshonna is a variation of the Hebrew name Shoshana, which means "lily or rose." My adoptive parents weren't Jewish; they were Baptist. So they changed my name to Shonna, which means "God is gracious." They believed I was a living example of my name, reminding me that God had shown favor over my life and theirs by putting us together.

Every year on my birthday, beginning when I was nine years old, I asked my adoptive parents for information on my birth parents. Every year I received the same answer. My birth records were closed, and they were not allowed access to them. They knew nothing of who my real parents were except that my mother was fifteen and my father was her nineteen year old boyfriend.

I was naturally a quiet child. I didn't keep up any trouble, and I didn't cause any problems. I followed the rules, did my chores, and kept my head in the books. I was a straight-A, honor roll, advanced placement, gifted student. I was a pleasant, obedient, delightful daughter. I qualified for seven different scholarships for college, which equaled a full-ride. I made the Dean's List. I graduated from high school with honors and Sum Cum Laude from college. I was in the National Honor Society and Who's Who Among American High School and College Students.

And look where I got me.

The job market was so bad in Memphis that neither Curtis nor I found jobs with our degrees after college. Yet, the year after we graduated, Curtis and I used our income tax returns to have a nice wedding with all of our closest family and friends. He had been my best friend, my prom date, my study buddy, and everything else I had ever needed him to be. All he asked was that I never stop being me. All I had to do was be his backbone, take care of his heart, keep him level-headed, and be the warmest, softest thing in his hard, cold world. All of those things came naturally to me.

I respected Curtis. I trusted him with my life; I loved him with every bit of my heart. I was not too proud of a woman to submit to my man. He was not too proud of a man to show open love, affection, and adoration for his woman. We had simple arguments that never lasted long, and we never went to bed mad at each other. We firmly believed in solving today's problems before they added to tomorrow's. We went out of our way to make each other happy. We were a perfect fit.

The day Curtis died, I knew I would never love any man the way I loved him. When he died, they buried three-fourths of my heart with him. I could never see myself trusting, loving, or submitting to another man the way I did with Curtis. My life as I knew it was over.

~ * ~ * ~ * ~

For some reason, when I found Curtis back in high school, I felt whole. Even when we were just friends, he made me happy. I felt like that piece of me that had been missing all of those years because I didn't know my birth parents had suddenly been found and the puzzle of my life was complete. I had stopped asking about my birth parents, and I'm sure it was much to my adoptive parents' relief. I had always vowed to find my biological parents when I turned eighteen, but with Curtis in my life, I had no desire to search for them. I had everything I needed in him.

So imagine my surprise sitting there in my living room when I opened that envelope and saw not one, but three copies of my original birth certificate. I couldn't begin to fathom what Curtis had done to obtain my birth certificate, but at that moment, Brad's words made all the sense in the world. "His method and his motive."

"Damn it, Curtis!" I sobbed. "God damn you!"

Chapter 6

The Letter

My Dear Sweet Wife Shonna,

If you are reading this, my life has come to its end. I cannot ask you not to cry for me because I know how much you love me. I expect you to cry. I expect you to grieve. I can only imagine the pain I would feel if I would have ever lost you. My mind can't even begin to fathom the depths of depression I would slip into without you. Grieve for me, My Love, but do not become depressed. We have loved each other truly and shall see each other again one day.

I refuse to attempt to serenade you with colloquial clichés to explain how I feel about you. Telling you that you are the air I breathe is a lie. If the next man's wife is the air he breathes then that phrase cannot begin to explain how I feel for you. You are not my air, nor my water. Neither are you my everything. Essentially, you are me, and I love you as such. You are a part of me, the very essence of me, and without you there definitely would be no me.

You're reading this letter, so obviously you've discovered my safe deposit box. Please enjoy its contents. There is much more for you to discover, and it's all for you. I know that nothing makes sense right now, and everything is extremely confusing. It's only going to get more unbelievable, but eventually it will all come together. Always remember, no matter what, that I love you and everything I did was to build a greater future for you, I, and any little blessings that would have come from our union. I hate to watch you work so hard and struggle to make ends meet, but once you uncover everything that is in store for you, you will see it was all worth it. Of course, money won't replace my love or my companionship, but when you get lonely and you miss me, just think of me. Remember my arms wrapped around you as we slept so many nights. Close your eyes and feel my body pressed against yours in the middle of the night.

No matter what happens, all I want is for you to be happy. You deserve happiness and so much more. Know that if it is at all possible, I will always be with you. I don't know what begins when life ends, but if the Lord allows, I will always watch over you, and when you need it most, listen for my voice just over your shoulder. Be happy, baby. Be wise with your choices and always be careful, as I am no longer here to protect you. Don't look for me in the stars; I am one man, not a constellation. Search for me in the wind when it blows almost invasively through your hair or caresses your cheek just a bit too familiarly. I am there. With you.

Love Always,

Your Husband Curtis

P. S. I have enclosed your birth certificate in the box as well. I searched high and low and finally was able to obtain it for you. Don't worry about how; just be sure to keep up with them. They did require several leaps and bounds and I'm sure I broke a few laws as well. It's all worth it for you. You need them. You can't understand who you are or figure out where you're headed unless you know where you've been.

Chapter 7

I was four months into the loneliness, and now I was dealing with an even more stressful issue. I had moved all of the bags and bundles of drugs and money into a bedroom in the new house. The smell of marijuana in the house had become so powerful and over-bearing that I just couldn't take it anymore. The blazing fireball of a Mid-South sun would come pouring into the high windows of the room and bake the weed. By the time I would return home from lunch or shopping or the spa, the entire house would smell like I was just wrapping up the world's largest smoke session.

One of the envelopes in the deposit box contained a list of Curtis' connects and clients. I made one phone call to the name at the top of the list. Big Bang. He was more than willing to take the goods off my hands when he found out I was Curtis' wife. The issue was that he thought he could get over on me. He tried to offer me six hundred dollars per pound for Kush. Even I knew that was bullshit. So I threatened to take my product elsewhere and sell it at top dollar. The drought in the city and Curtis' reputation for having only top-quality product made Big Bang sing a different tune. He bought half of my weed on the spot.

My first time going to the new house, I had discovered the Audi R8 and the Range Rover in the garage. I called it my delivery van. When I went on big shopping sprees, I'd drive the Range to make sure I had enough room for all of my bags. When I made the first deal with Big Bang, I loaded up half of my weed in the Range Rover to deliver it to him. I backed the truck up to his garage and waited with the gun Curtis had left in the nightstand on my lap as Big Bang's goons unloaded the packages. Big Bang hopped into my passenger seat as they worked.

"You do business like your husband," he told me. "He never brought you around, though. Was he teaching you in the background?"

"I learned from my husband's mistakes," I replied simply.

"That's wise. I see he's taught you well. He must've made a lot of mistakes," he chuckled. "I understand why you have your strap on your lap, so I won't take offense to it. I want you to realize, though, that you're safe around me. Nothing's going to happen to you. If Curtis were here, he'd be able to vouch that I'm good people," he told me.

"Well, Curtis isn't here, and I don't know you from a can of paint. All I know is what I've experienced for myself. You just made a rather sizable purchase from me at a fair price after trying to hustle me and give me pennies for my dollars."

"Easy, Slim. It's all in business. I just had to see what kind of game we were playing so I'd know what my position was."

"Well, for future reference, I'm not playing any games cuz niggas don't play fair. Just remember: I'll always win because bullets take all."

His eyes got large for a second as he stared at me. I faced forward and allowed my words to sink into his head and saturate his thoughts.

"Well, you have my sincerest condolences. I'mma just leave this on your back seat," he said as he lifted a blue backpack.

"Naw, you can hand that here," I told him.

He handed it to me, and I thumbed through the money. I counted the money twice before I looked up at him with narrowed eyes.

"Mother fucker, I see you really think this shit is a game," I said as I cocked my gun and put the hole to his chin. "I just sold you twenty-two pounds of Kush and you thought I wasn't gone count my shit?" Big Bang looked at me with the fear of God in his eyes. Man or boy, old or young, ugly or sexy, nigga or gentleman, every member of the male species knows when to fear a woman, and obviously Big Bang had realized this was one of those moments.

"Just…just hold on, Slim," he said with his hands up.

"Naw, ain't no fucking hold on!" I told him. "What was the agreement?" He remained silent. "What was the mother fucking agreement?!" I yelled as I shoved the gun deeper into his chin.

"Twenty-two pounds of grade-A gas at forty-five hundred a pound."

"Say it again. I couldn't hear you," I said maniacally.

"Twenty-two pounds of grade-A gas for forty-five hundred a pound," he repeated.

"How many times did I have you repeat this back to me on the phone?" I quizzed him.

"Three times," he mumbled.

"What? Speak up!"

"Three times."

"Can you count?"

"Yeah," he said with a quivering voice.

"So why am I short nine thousand dollars? Correct me if I'm wrong, but forty-five hundred times twenty-two is ninety-nine thousand, isn't it?"

"Yeah, it is."

"So instead of throwing an extra thousand into the bag to make it an even hundred thousand... you know, for my gas and delivery and just to be a gentleman to a beautiful woman with whom you're conducting a business transaction for the first time... you decided to short me nine thousand? What you thought this was? A restaurant? You just gone take a tip, huh?" I was pissed, and I knew he could see the fire in my eyes.

"I- I was just ch-checking, Slim. Th-that's all. I- I got the rest of your money," he stuttered.

"Where the fuck is it and why the fuck it ain't in my bag?"

"It-it's in the house. I can go get it for you. It's all a part of the business, Slim. I was trying to see if you were on top of your shit. That's all. You know how it is. Get or be gotten. Eat or get eaten."

"You're crazy as hell if you think I'm about to let you climb your fat ass out of this truck and go in that house without my money being in my hand," I laughed at his dumb ass. "You ain't got my nine racks in your pocket?" He shook his head. "So you were dead ass serious about shorting my shit?"

"My bad, Shawty. For real."

"You'd better get your ass on the phone and call and tell one of those niggas to bring my shit out the front door, and I mean right fucking now," I said through gritted teeth. He pulled his phone out of his pocket.

"Hey, Goose... yeah, I need you to look in the stash and bring Slim the rest of the money in the blue envelope. Yeah, should be nine racks..."

"Oh, no," I stopped him. "See, I charge a fee for the inconvenience." He looked taken aback. "See, we had a clear understanding on our agreement. You chose to violate the terms of the agreement, so now you owe me fifteen thousand instead of just nine," I told him. "And I still expect you to throw in my extra band for my gas and delivery." I gave him a wide, pretty smile and cat eyes as I hurt his feelings.

"Yeah, Goose...look in the green envelope and peel Slim off seven extra bands...Yeah, I know...Look, just do what I say, aight?!...And hurry the fuck up!"

"I really hate you brought this kind of tension and distrust into this relationship, Bang. My intentions were to do continued business with you. I had hopes that you'd be a repeat customer. Tsk tsk," I shook my head overly dramatically. "Now, I don't know. Seems like too much of a hassle."

"Naw, Shawty. Ain't no hassle. We good."

"Shit, I gotta threaten you and post you up just to get what you owe me. Do I look like I have the patience to do this shit every time we conduct a transaction?"

"I'm saying, it's the first time I've ever conducted business with you. I had to find out if you were a pluck or not," he tried to explain.

"You're right about one thing: it is the first time we've conducted a transaction," I told him. "But you know what they say about first impressions, right?" I raised an eyebrow at him. "So far you've fucked that up. My first impression of you is that you're a liar, a thief, and a snake. Your work is just as sloppy as your appearance, judging by the three inch gap between the bottom of your garage door and the floor of the garage, especially given that your crew just unloaded a whole fed charge into that same garage."

"You're right. We got off on the wrong foot. I accept responsibility for that. That's my bad. I apologize," he said.

"If you really want to make it up to me, you'll have your guy hurry the fuck up! Run me my mother fucking money so I can roll," I said as I pushed the gun deeper into the soft flesh under his chin. He immediately picked up his cell phone again.

"Aye, yo, Goose. Man, hurry the fuck up, man. Slim ain't playing, man... I don't care! Hurry the fuck up!"

A few minutes later, Goose approached the passenger door carrying an envelope. He handed it to Big Bang through the window and went back inside. Big Bang started to hand me the envelope.

"Now, Bang," I started, "ain't no third or fourth chances. You sure you wanna hand me this envelope without counting the contents first?"

"You're right, Ms. Lady. Let me thumb through it real quick just to be on the safe side." He licked his thumb and in-dex finger with a white-coated tongue, and my flesh crawled. I watched as he counted out sixteen thousand dollars. "It's all here, Slim. Here you go," he said as he handed me the enve-lope.

"It'd better be," I said as I recounted the money. It was all there. I dropped the envelope in the bag with the rest of the money and then turned back to Big Bang.

"See, no worries, Slim. I'm going to do right by you," he said.

"Get out of my car, Bang."

"We good or what?"

"Get your ass out of my car, you fat fuck. You better pray

I even consider doing business with you again after the bull-shit you just put me through."

"Aye, you ain't finna be talking to me crazy and shit," he tried to amp up on me.

"Oh, yeah?" I said as I put the hole of my gun to the tip of his nose. "How about I stop you from talking at all? How about I silence your mother fucking ass?"

"Alright, Slim. I'm gone. I'm out," he said. He grabbed the door handle and opened the door. In my rear view mirror, I saw Big Bang stand at his front door and watch me drive away.

Chapter 8

I had named my house "Igloo Knox" for two reasons: every inch of the property showed that my husband was a cold mother fucker, and the whole damn place was as secure as Rikers and San Quentin. A ten foot tall brick wall surrounded the entire five acres of land. The house itself was constructed in the exact middle of the property so intruders or visitors could be seen coming before they reached the house itself. There was an unused basketball court, tennis court, swimming pool, and even a playground area.

I had spent my free time trying to dodge boredom by exploring the new house, blue prints in hand. No one knew where I lived, including my mom and my friends. None of Curtis' family even knew about this place. A few nights after I had met up with Big Bang, while walking through the house, I made a shocking discovery.

It started with a squeaky floorboard. A squeaky floorboard in a brand new house was just a bit too curious for me. I stood back and examined the hardwood floor in one of the downstairs bedrooms after hearing the sound beneath my right foot. I'll never forget. It was one forty-two in the morning when I found my husband's stash.

I opened the flap I found beneath the Persian rug in the bedroom. There was a full staircase- not a ladder or a set of wooden basement steps- that led down into a room the size of a living room. Shelves lined the walls, three rows of shelving stood in the middle of the floor, and a long table was against the far wall.

Everything about the room built underneath the house said "Fed Charge." If this was what Glenn and Lil Don had been looking for, they were crazy if they thought this stuff was even able to fit in our little bitty ass house.

Curtis had shit in that room that I had never even heard of. The weed was packaged in pounds, the cocaine in kilos. There were what looked like pickle jars that were labeled and full of prescription pills lined up on the shelves. Boxes of Suboxone strips lined the top shelves of two sets of shelving, and I had no clue what they even were.

"Look at all of this!" I whispered out loud to myself. "It's so organized... but it's so much shit! How am I going to get rid of all of this stuff?" I asked myself as I slowly walked through the room, taking it all in. I was no drug dealer and had never aspired to be one, but I had come to realize that it was an area in which I was actually very talented. The problem was that I knew next to nothing about the pricing and packaging of the shit I was selling and even less about the shit Curtis had stored in the drug lair.

It didn't take anything at all for me to Google the Suboxone strips and the different pills to see what they were and what they were used for, but you can't Google the street value of an entire box or bottle of that kind of stuff. Plus, I was still concerned that using a search engine to research that kind of stuff on my phone would leave a paper trail exposing my affairs.

I looked up from my phone as I lay in bed that night to stare at the picture of Curtis and me he had hanging on the wall over the dresser. I had all the money I could ever hope for, more money I had yet to discover, and the means to multiply it all… and yet, it meant nothing without that one person to share it with. The money couldn't bring Curtis back or buy my happiness. I had this big beautiful house, another one I hadn't even seen yet, cars that couldn't even be called cars. They were more like vehicles… automobiles. And yet, Curtis was gone, and we had no children. I was all alone. It was the middle of the night that was the worst- when he wasn't there but my thoughts of him were.

I stared at our faces in the photograph. We were so happy. Our smiles were wide and our love was evident. He was holding me close to him at the moment the photographer snapped the picture, I remembered. My back was to his chest and his arms were wrapped tightly around me. All I remembered thinking at that moment was how safe I felt in his arms, how genuine I knew the picture would look, how much I loved my husband.

My heart dropped. I was twenty-seven. I was a widow. I was lonely, horny, and even though I had every material thing my heart desired, I was miserable. Tears filled my eyes as I stared at my husband's pearly white smile. What I wouldn't give to feel his strong arms around me just once more. Just to hear his laugh or feel his fingertips slap my ass one more time… To roll over in the middle of the night and feel him snuggled beneath me.

I sighed heavily and decided to turn in for the night. I dropped to my knees next to the bed and said the same prayer

I said every night. Lately, I had been asking God to bless my husband's soul and forgive me for my drug-dealing sins. That night, in addition to all of that, I asked God to ease the pain of loneliness in my heart.

~ * ~ * ~ * ~

My answer came two lonely nights later in the form of a bling from my Messenger app. I had just set up a run to drop off three pounds of weed, a kilo of cocaine, half a box of Suboxone strips, and one hundred each of four different types of pills to a guy named Darrel who was second on Curtis' list, just beneath Big Bang. When I called him, Darrel had explained that the merchandise he picked up was run as contraband to both the Shelby County Jail and the Shelby County Penal Farm. He would drop all of the items, along with several packages of tobacco, off with Corrections Officers to take into the facilities and distribute to inmates who had paid for them by having family members drop off money with him. The Corrections Officers would pick up the items and receive a hefty fee for their services- a fee meant to compensate them for the risk they ran of losing their jobs if caught.

I was already in shock from receiving and digesting that information as I counted out pills and packaged them in Zip Lock bags at the table in my husband's Drug Lair when the familiar sound came from my cell phone as it lay on the corner of the table. I finished packaging the oxycodone I was working on before I removed my latex gloves and picked up the phone.

Good evening, Beautiful, the message read. I was always leery of random inbox messages from men I didn't know. It wasn't like I wasn't aware that I was beautiful. My light complexion, hour glass shape, and almond-shaped eyes would attract Stevie Wonder. But the profile photo on this man's page caused me to do a double-take.

This man was about six feet tall, one hundred eighty pounds, chocolate-skinned, and sculpted like a statue. He was beautiful. The more I scrolled through his photos, the more awestruck I became. His profile said he was single and living in Memphis.

Hey handsome

He read the message instantly. I stared at his picture as I watched the bubbles indicate he was typing. Where the hell did he come from? I wondered. We had no mutual friends.

Saw a beautiful face and thought I'd speak. I've been watching you for a while.

I was kind of creeped out by the fact that he had been watching me and hadn't said anything, but I shrugged it off, thinking I took it the wrong way. I told myself I should proba-bly be flattered.

You're not half-stepping yourself. Thanx for the com-pliment tho.

TY. We should get together some time when you're available.

When I'm available? I thought to myself. So his avail-ability is open? I scrolled through his profile again. It didn't say anything about a job, but then again, we weren't Facebook friends. I thought that maybe I couldn't see it because of his security settings on his page.

> *Maybe during the weekend? I work during the week.*

It wasn't a whole lie. It just wasn't the whole truth either. I giggled at it myself.

> *This weekend?*

> *Idk. Idk u like that.*

> *We'll get to know each other some & then set something up. How does that sound?*

> *Sounds good.*

He seemed harmless enough, but I knew I could never be too careful. I had begun to get used to being alone and knew that no one was going to look out for me and my safety more than I would myself.

> *What's your stats?*

> *Female, black, 27, single, no kids. U?*

> *Male, black (obviously), 25, single, no kids*

> *You're 25?*

> *Yep.*

U look older. Like maybe 30.

Is that bad?

No, I just meant u look mature.

Well ty. R u busy? Am I interrupting u?

I looked around at the packages I had stacked on the table. Everything was ready for transport and delivery.

Nah, not really

Let me ask u a few questions then

We were up all night until nine-thirty the next morning talking about nearly everything. I say nearly because of course I dodged all questions about where I lived and my occupation or anything about my source of income. I knew better than to give him too much information or to trust him too much. I used to trust people until they gave me a reason not to do so. I had learned, though, that in this business- in most businesses, as a matter of fact- you'd better not trust anyone at all. That rule applied to some people even after they've proven themselves trustworthy.

Maximillian Williams III had neither proven himself trustworthy or not, but he had proven himself to possess an exceptional amount of intellect. H was well-studied in politics and current affairs. He was well-learned in African American history, literature, music, and movements. He was neither blinded by the lies, charades, and facades of the government or any other public entities, nor overly enthusiastic due to the outbursts, riots, and marches of our people in the recent years. He was… awake.

And I felt relieved and refreshed. It had been so long since I had held an intelligent and meaningful conversation with anyone that he truly had my eyes open and my curiosity piqued. I enjoyed our conversation that first night and every night after for three months before I even considered meeting him in person.

Chapter 9

"Look at you," he uttered quietly, his amazement slathered across his face like butter on a roll. He extended his hand to help me up the front steps of the restaurant. "You look amazing."

"Thank you," I said as I smiled just enough to show my appreciation, but not enough to reveal just how flattered I actually was. "You look handsome yourself," I told him, "and you smell incredible."

"Well, thank you," he said as he held open the door of Pappadeux Seafood Restaurant. My simple black Jimmy Choos clicked against the tile floor as we approached the hostess.

"Williams reservation for two," he told the young blonde who looked as though she was no older than a college Sophomore. My own insecurities got the best of me as I studied the young woman. As much of an air as I was putting on, I had never been to a nice restaurant, and as sophisticated as I appeared, I was more than humble.

I surveyed the other diners as the hostess escorted us to our table. My black Chanel dress fit right in with the other women. Max waited for me to take my seat before sitting down himself. I'll never forget that night. He was wearing a light blue button down and navy blue slacks pressed and creased precisely, a Rolex, and beautiful diamond studs in both ears. He had a fresh haircut and his cologne had him smelling absolutely edible.

56 -Slim Thick

I had told Max I had business to tend to in Atlanta, which was why we met there. He had already been there for three days visiting with family. The business I had to handle was collecting the contents of Curtis' safe deposit box at a bank there, and in true Curtis fashion, it was well worth the trip. In the trunk of the Audi R8, I had a Victoria's Secret tote with sixty thousand dollars, six pairs of diamond and gold earrings, seven men's chains, and the titles to a Porsche 911 and an Aston Martin Vantage GT zipped up inside.

I must have fallen in love with Max that night while we talked over dinner, wine, and dessert. He was already physically stunning, and his words sounded amazing as I watched his lips speak them. The intellectual level on which we connected only enhanced our mutual sexual attraction to each other.

The wine had me tipsy, so Max followed me back to the Ritz Carlton where I had an executive suite, and I invited him up to chill for a few minutes before he returned to his own room at the Four Seasons. Why did I do that?

We stopped the cars at the front door of the hotel and the valets opened our doors. I looked back at him, eying him seductively…inviting him. He got out of his Benz and handed the valet the key, and then followed behind me, watching my hips sway as my heels click-clacked against the lobby's tile floor. I stepped into the elevator and then waited for him to enter as well before pushing my floor on the panel.

I stared straight ahead as if my flesh wasn't burning from his eyes piercing the side of my face. I caught a glimpse of him out of the corner of my eye that made me turn and look at him directly. He wasn't just staring at me; he was admiring me. His eyes were slightly glossed over as if he had zoned out, and yet, they were scanning my body, notating, calculating.

He stepped closer to me as the elevator approached my floor and the scent of his cologne flowed into my nostrils and found its home somewhere near the butterflies in my stomach. The elevator rang as it stopped and Max placed his palm on the small of my back, ushering me out of the elevator.

I took careful steps at a steady pace as we walked the carpeted hallway to my room. Max followed closely behind me, and all I could do was pray to God that I didn't make an ass of myself by twisting my ankle in these heels while I was trying to walk sexy. The last thing I needed was for my ankle to snap to the side and look like a fool in front of the first man to show me some attention since my husband was killed. Men really get a kick out of seeing a woman's ankle snap like that.

When we got into the room, he excused himself to the bathroom, and I slipped out of my heels, sat on the edge of the bed, and turned on the TV. I was nervous, but anxious at the same time. I knew what time it was. There wasn't any sitting and talking. That man had pure lust in his eyes and I knew he was about to make a move on me, and I fully planned to let him. I gave him a cute little smile as he came out of the bathroom. Max walked over to me, grabbed my hand and pulled me to my feet, lifted my head with his hand on my cheek, and then pressed his lips firmly, but gently against mine.

I instantly surrendered as my body gave in to him. It was like drinking wine for the first time: the unsure feeling of if you're ready for what you're doing and if it's right, and the sweet satisfaction of obtaining something you've desired and anticipated for a long time. I exhaled deeply as he pulled away from the kiss. Unzipping my dress, Max slipped it over my shoulders and watched it fall to my feet as he ran his hands over my shoulders, down to my ass, and then pulled me close and kissed me again. I unbuttoned his shirt and opened it as he rubbed his dick against me. He was rock hard and his dick was down his leg. That was all I needed to know.

I pulled his shirt off and then yanked his tank top over his head as well. He was cut. I mean, he had washboard abs like he had been in the gym religiously. He unsnapped my bra, my breasts tumbled out, and he grabbed my left breast, bent down, and wrapped his lips around it.

It had been months since I had felt a man's touch, let alone a man's lips anywhere on my body. So when he laid me down on the bed, removed my thong, and ran his tongue in circles over my pussy, my body screamed out in relief. My hands involuntarily pushed his face deeper into my wetness and he eagerly obliged. He pushed my legs wide open, which in turn spread the flesh between my legs, and he licked stronger, deeper. His tongue darted in and out, and my back arched as I released a deep moan that turned into what was almost a wail.

Satisfied with his work, Max stood over me, unbuckled his pants, and allowed them to fall to the floor with his boxers. My jaw dropped. Perhaps I had been with Curtis too long because Max's dick was huge by my standards. I moved backwards on the bed and Max climbed over me and kissed me again, deeply, passionately. I melted into the sheets as he slid himself inside of me and my body sighed in relief.

Max stroked slowly, looking back and forth between my eye sand where we were connected at the center. Then he lifted one of my legs into the crook of his arm and stroked even deeper. The heat between us was so intense it didn't feel like we were touching the stars. It felt like the stars had come down to meet us on my bed. My voice quivered as it attempted to moan. My fingers trembled as they attempted to touch him, and I was lost in the ecstasy of having him inside of me as my hips gyrated in unison with his stroke to meet him at the center. He bent lower, flicked his tongue over my nipple, and then engulfed it with his lips, pulling back on it gently.

I was so lost in my own pleasure I didn't realize how good it felt to Max. His eyes closed as he moaned in sync with his strokes. When he finally opened his eyes, he looked at me and then kissed me again. Pulling me to the edge of the bed, he stood up and stroked it from a standing position, but then pulled me to my feet, spun me around, and bent me over.

"Hold on to the legs of the chair," he told me. I was apprehensive at first, but did as I was instructed and almost lost my mind as Max dug deep inside of me like he was trying to touch my soul. I tightened my calf muscles and locked the arch in my back as he held my hips and pounded me from behind. His dick throbbed inside of me as I lifted up some to be bent over and began throwing it back to meet his thrusts.

I suddenly stood straight up and, with my back against his chest, rolled my hips on his hardness. I turned around and grabbed his hands, sat him down in the chair, bent over, and twerked on his dick. He slid it back inside of me as I continued to twerk and he slapped my ass cheeks as they jumped.

"Oh God," he moaned as I bounced on his lap. When I sat up, grabbed the arms of the chair, and swirled my hips in his lap, I thought he'd lose his mind. At that moment, I could tell he had a sudden epiphany. He realized that I couldn't be in charge. I couldn't lead the dance. Every move I made in every position was with professional precision and it would always feel like the most perfect stroke.

I leaned back as I turned around and put my legs over his shoulders. Gripping my hips tightly, Max stood up and fucked me in mid-air, issuing hard thrusts that resounded throughout the room. I moaned loudly as my grip tightened on his triceps and that familiar feeling began to inch its way from the arch of my feet up through my knee caps and then my breastbone. Pinning me against the wall, Max pumped forcefully, with short, strong grunts accompanying each blow. He looked into my eyes into a place past my pupils and witnessed my pleasure growing, my orgasm drawing near. He pumped and pumped until suddenly I exploded, my juices drenching his dick, forcing him over the top into his own orgasmic extravagance.

With me still in his arms, Max turned and laid me on the bed and then collapsed next to me breathing heavily. We lay there, both of us trying to steady our breathing and stabilize our heartrates. I looked over at him lying there with his eyes closed, his breathing becoming a bit heavier, his body getting just a bit too comfortable.

It was three in the morning. As in love with the dick as I was, I had strict rules. There was no such thing as spending the night- whether at my house or at a hotel. His sex was the bomb and his conversation was banging, but I still didn't know him well enough to close my eyes with him lying next to me. I looked over at him breathing hard and getting ready to doze off. I think not! I thought to myself. I cleared my throat. When that didn't get his attention, I nudged him in his side with my elbow.

"What's up, baby?" he asked as he peeked on eye open at me.

"You probably want to get a towel and get cleaned up before you leave," I told him. Was I too blunt? Maybe I should've been nicer about it or hinted at it. Either way, he still had to roll.

"You don't want me to keep you company tonight? Keep you warm?"

"Ummm, nah. I don't like a lot of... umm... people around me when I'm sleep."

"A lot of people? There's nobody in here but me, baby. But if you're ready for me to leave, I understand. I can take a hint. I can get down with the pounce and bounce," he said. He was lying. His feelings were hurt. I could tell. He expected to have me wide open after that slaying and instead he was a pothole on a Memphis street after it snows: He was busted open, only getting wider, and nobody was getting around to him anytime soon.

"It's not like that, Max," I started, but he cut me off.

"Naw, Slim. It's cool. I understand. Where's the bathroom?" he said as he rose from the bed and ran his hand over his waves.

"To the left." I laughed at my own joke as I sang the Beyonce' song in my head.

The moment I heard the bathroom door click closed and the water running, I sprang into action. Snatching my phone off the nightstand, I turned on the camera, swiped his billfold from the floor next to his pants, and took pictures of his driver's license, social security card, and the front and back of two credit cards and two bank cards. As soon as the water cut off, I stuck the billfold back beneath his pants and flew back onto the bed. "The hands are quicker than the eyes" I had heard someone say once. In this case, maybe "timing is everything" was more appropriate.

Chapter 10

From that day forward, Max and I were damn-near inseparable. He would go to work every day and I would handle my business trying to get rid of the illegal content of my husband's basement, but every little bit of free time we could scrape up was spent together. I found myself at Max's Collierville mansion at least four days a week. I still was not comfortable enough to spend the night and I had yet to even allow Max to know where I lived, but that all came to a head two months after our rendezvous in Atlanta.

Max and I had an arrangement. We were not in a committed relationship, which was solely my idea. Max actually preferred that we become a couple, but I had just gotten out of a relationship in the worst way and I still felt I needed more time to heal from the loss of my husband. Max and I would have sex whenever either of us desired, which was all the time. We would hang out and Max's house and he would cook dinner or order out. We would Netflix and chill, YouTube and chill, Xfinity and chill, but we never went out anywhere to be seen together in public. I was still doubtful of Max's staying power, especially if he found out how I made my money or even my net worth, and I didn't want to have to deal with Curtis' friends and family criticizing and complaining about my new beau if they found out. I had almost completely disconnected myself from all of my friends and family as well as Curtis'. No one knew where I lived. No one had seen me in months.

This particular Saturday, I had set up multiple drops for delivery during the day so that they wouldn't interfere with the dinner plans Max and I had for that night. Trying to stay on schedule, I made a drop with Big Bang's goon Goose, who I had discovered was actually his brother, and had collected payment without incident. I had also made two smaller drops with some small-time street corner dope boys from one of Curtis' lists. I had a bit of time between drops, so I stopped at a little lingerie shop I had discovered in Mid-Town Memphis to do some browsing. I was getting ready to check out when Darrel texted me that he was doing another pick-up in about thirty minutes and asked if I could meet him at the same location so he could handle it all at one time. It seemed fair enough, so I had him text me the location, and when I paid for my garter belt and stockings I headed to the Wolfchase Galleria Mall to meet him at the back of the parking lot.

Over the months I had learned that things go a lot more unnoticed if you do them in the open. People tend to think nothing of what you're doing if you have the demeanor like you're not doing anything wrong, out of the ordinary, or unusual. When you try to hide down a back street or if you're looking around to see who's watching, you appear suspicious. It doesn't matter what crime you're committing. If you look like you're doing nothing more than minding your own business, people tend to overlook you and mind their own business as well. For this reason, most of my transactions were conducted in broad daylight during normal business hours in public places. It was bold, but it was the smartest piece of my operation.

I smiled at Darrel as I pulled up next to his dinosaur of a BMW. He was a sweetheart. He was young and all about his money. He couldn't have been a day older than twenty, and most of the Corrections Officers he delivered to were his cousins and people he grew up with in the hood. The BMW was a car he bought from his grandmother and he lived in a one bedroom apartment in a middle-class neighborhood and rarely had visitors. It's amazing what a little money could do...like put a private investigator on my payroll.

I put the delivery van in park, popped the trunk, and got out. I lifted the back hatch and uncovered the boxes I had packaged in the back.

"What's up, Momma?" Darrel greeted me as he got out of his car. "How you been?"

"I've been just fine. How has business been?"

"Well, you know. Business is business," he said as he shrugged it off.

I slid the box that belonged to him closer to the edge of the trunk as he chatted. When he saw the box, he turned and reached into his car. My instincts kicked in, and I upped my 40 out of my jeans and had it pointed at his face before he could even turn back around.

"Slim, what the fuck?!" he said when he did. "What you doing, Momma?!" He damn-near pissed his pants when he saw that big ass hole aimed at his nose. My eyes darted down and caught sight of the yellow envelope in his hand and my adrenaline rush instantly ceased.

"Damn it, D, man! Don't be making no sudden moves like that! Shit!" I said as I popped the bullet out of the chamber and dropped it in my pocket.

"You thought I was reaching for a gun? Damn, Slim, man. I thought you knew me better than that. You know I ain't that type of nigga. I ain't no stick up kid," Darrel said. I could tell I had scared the shit out of him, but I had hurt his feelings too.

"My bad, Darrel," I said more calmly as I slipped the gun back into my jeans, "But you used to do business with my husband. I know you think I should know you better than that, but I was with my husband for ten years and never knew he was doing this shit. I thought I knew him better than that. This is business, man. You have to stay on your toes."

"Naw, Ma," he shook his head. "Them six inch Jimmy Choos you got on keep you on your toes. I haven't given you any reason to be on pens and needles around me. I operate on the trust system. We're both committing crimes here. We have to be able to trust each other."

"I know, sweetheart. It's not you. It's me. And you're completely right. I want you to remember this too though: This is not the business to trust everybody in. Trust no man until he proves he can be trusted. That should be one of your top rules. Trust no nigga. Remember that shit because not remembering it can get you killed." He nodded at me in understanding.

"I got you," he said as he looked me in my eyes.

"Didn't you say you were meeting somebody else here too? Where's he at?" I asked as I handed Darrel his box.

"He's running late," he said, "but here he comes now."

Darrel nodded toward a car coming around the bend. I turned and looked and my jaw dropped. Darrel was trying to put the envelope in my hand, but my fingers wouldn't close around it. My heart was in my stomach and my stomach was in my knees. I was about to fall the fuck out.

Max whipped up in front of Darrel's car in the flyest Challenger I had ever seen. Tinted windows, chrome kit, pipes… It was obvious the mother fucker was running. Max had the driver's side window down and was rocking a pair of Bvlgari sunglasses that I knew cost about seventeen hundred dollars. There was nowhere for me to hide, and even if there were, I was frozen in place and I was sure he had spotted me from a mile away.

"Shonna," he exhaled.

"Max," I whimpered.

"Shonna, what the fuck is going on here? What the fuck are you doing here?" he said as he threw open the car door and got out.

"Max, I can explain…" I started.

"You two know each other?" Darrel frowned.

"Explain what, Shonna? How? This shit looks pretty crystal clear to me!" Max crossed his arms.

"Nigga, you're screaming and fussing at me while I should be cursing you out."

"What?"

"What happened to your damn job, Max? Aren't you supposed to be at work?" I huffed and then crossed my arms across my chest.

"Yeah, well, this is work. This is my job. This is my career, my occupation," he said resolutely.

"Umm, I don't mean to interrupt, but what the fuck is going on here?" Darrel's eyes darted back and forth between the two of us.

"So you're a drug dealer?" I asked Max.

"So you're a drug dealer?" he returned the question. "Hell, you're fussing at me and your ass is out her slanging shit too."

"It's not what you think, baby."

"It's not what I think? What's in the box, Shonna? Huh? What's in the fucking box?!" he yelled. I had never seen Max angry before. We had never even had an argument. Yet, here we were having our first one, and, boy, it was a hell of an argument.

"It's not what you think, Max. Okay? You don't under-stand," I said firmly.

"Well make me understand then, Shonna! I'm out here thinking you're a good girl who works a legitimate job and lives a quiet life. I'm spending all this time with you, thinking about changing my whole lifestyle for you, and you're out here doing the same shit I'm doing!"

"Uhh, maybe I should go…" Darrel said.

"No, our business is conducted here, Darrel. I'll go. You can finish what you have to handle with your friend here," I said to Darrel without taking my eyes off Max's pupils.

"Don't you walk away from me, Shonna," Max warned.

"Whatever, Max. I'll get up with you later." I shooed him off over my shoulder like a fly.

"Shonna," he said as he grabbed my arm to stop me.

"You'd better get your hands off me," I said through gritted teeth.

"You're not about to just walk away from me like I'm not talking about shit."

"Maximillian," I said very quietly, "this is not the time or the place. You need to let go of my arm, check your surroundings, finish up whatever it is you had to do here, and clear this parking lot." Max's eyes darted around, catching sight of a group of old white women standing next to a Lincoln Town Car staring in our direction. His fingers released his grip on my arm and I closed the trunk of my truck.

"I expect you tonight for dinner," he said to my back.

70 – Slim Thick

I looked back at him as I opened my door, then got in and drove away.

~ * ~ * ~ * ~

I had fucked up and I knew it, and Max knew he had fucked up too. He called my phone every thirty minutes the rest of the day, but I didn't answer even once. When I missed dinner, he started texting me as well.

7:44   *So you're just going to ignore me?*

8:26   *This what we've come to? U can't even answer me?*

8:49   *Shonna*

9:27   *Shonna I'm sorry for lying to u. U lied to me 2*

9:56   *Shonna can we at least talk about this?*

10:33   *Baby I said I'm sorry*

11:04   *Shonna I'm not finna beg u. I cooked dinner & had to eat alone. This shit is wrong.*

11:18   *Damn Shonna. Wtf?*

11:51   *So this how u wanna play? Bet.*

After all of that time, I finally decided to text him back.

12:03   *I'm sorry too, Max. For lying to u & hiding this from u. There's a good reason for everything I do. Just always know that I always have your best interest at heart.*

12:07   *Whatever Shonna. Come thru tomorrow for dinner so we can talk. We both owe each other an explanation.*

12:09   *I'll be there at 6. I'm cooking. Dinner will be at 8.*

12:13   *Ok*

Chapter 11

I dreaded going to Max's house that evening, but I figured I'd better get it over with instead of drawing it out. Either Max would accept me as I was and I'd accept him, or we'd go our separate ways. It was as simple as that.

I went to the grocery store and grabbed all of the ingredients I needed to make Kansas City Steak- one of my specialties. I even decided to bake a cake- one of the simplest cakes I've ever made, but certainly one of the most delicious.

When I got to Max's house at noon, he wasn't there, which was perfect for me. I let myself in with the spare key to drop off the groceries and then went back home. I knew that Max would come home sometime before 6, so I wanted to leave the groceries so he'd know for sure I was coming back. We may have been at odds, but I didn't want to stress him out. Relationship or not, I still cared about him.

I sat in the tub and soaked, eyes closed, head back. Max was catching feelings for me. I could tell. He had made it clear from the very beginning that he wanted to be in a relationship with me, but all of the time we had been spending together had him falling for me. I knew Max would forgive me. He probably already had. I certainly couldn't hold his activities against me, given that I was twice as deep in the same business.

It had been a while since Max and I had had sex. My little lingerie collection had been growing, but going unused. My refusal to spend the night at Max's house had been putting a strain on our friendship and forming a wedge between us. We'd have dinner and talk all night until we were tired, but by the time Max would make a move on me, it would always be very late and time for me to leave and head home.

But tonight…there was something different about tonight. It was like that moment when your lips are pressed against the warm juicy lips of a man you've been talking to for months. That moment when your juices are flowing and the speed of your breathing increases, when your heart begins to race in anticipation. That moment when you're trying your best to fight the urge, the need, that terrible aching desire. When you're nervous, scared, insecure because you've never disrobed in front of this man, though you've contemplated it numerous time, and you're in the midst of that moment.

I had already made love to Max. Max and I had made love so sweet that it would put the ripest peach and the freshest honeycomb to shame. Our love making would make porn stars blush and married couples jealous. We fucked like we were in love and made love like we didn't give a fuck. And yet, I had never spent the night.

Max had already uncovered my big secret. He was already inside, whether I had opened the door and let him in or he had barged his way in or simply stumbled upon an open door. He was in there either way. I was already naked with my legs spread. I might as well just lay back and let go. This was the rationale that I used as I packed my black satin Victoria's Secret bag in preparation to be away from home for the rest of the night. Let go.

Letting go was such a hard thing to do. I had still not

let go of my hopes and prayers that Curtis would one day peek his head around the corner and into the door of the bedroom as I slept at night. I still had not let go of the thought that my biological mother would one day desire to have some sort of relationship with me and seek me out. So it took me forever to let go and let Max inside- to surrender to him.

I sat on the edge of my bed for an hour thinking things over and reminding myself that at some point I was going to have to take a chance on love if I didn't want to spend the rest of my life alone. I looked up at the picture of Curtis and me hanging on the wall. The tears fell without notice.

"God damn you, Curtis!" I screamed. "Why'd you do this to me? Why'd you leave me here like this? Look what you've done to me!"

He simply smiled back with the same loving smile frozen in time that I had fallen asleep staring at every night. I longed to hear his voice, his laugh, his heartbeat. I hadn't even gotten to say goodbye. They had scraped my husband up off the floor of our home, slicked him up, tossed him in a casket, and buried him deep…all while I was being starved, beaten, and tortured in an abandoned warehouse where Curtis' killers were now rotting away.

I swiped the tears from my cheeks, aggravated by my own vulnerability and disappointed by Curtis' mortality. I was tired of taking things slow, being careful, being a good girl. I went into my walk-in closet and examined my body in my nakedness in the full-length mirror. I was beautiful, even with my eyes slightly red and puffy. My plump and perky D-cups over my thin waist that preluded my apple-bottom booty all came together to form a figure most women would kill for. I smiled slightly as I looked into the hints of green in the midst of the hazel brown of my eyes. Baby, whatever it was that niggas were looking for, I had it.

I dried my eyes with a Chanel scarf and looked at myself again. That was it. I was all in.

"Fuck how it turn out," I told my reflection.

~ * ~ * ~

"So we're just going to sit here and let the elephant control the room?" Max stared at me over the rim of his glass of wine.

"I haven't eaten all day, Max. Can we eat? We're going to talk. It's not like we're avoiding each other," I told him as I scooped some mashed potatoes up with some steak and gravy and then slid it into my mouth.

"Shonna-"

"Is the food good?" I cut him off.

"Yeah, of course, but-"

"Well eat before it gets cold. We have plenty of time to talk."

Max cleaned his plate, had seconds, and then cut himself a slice of cake and sat on the living room sofa to wait for me in front of the TV. I sighed as I rose from the table and loaded the dish washer, taking my time as I tried to get my thoughts together.

"This cake is delicious," he said as I walked into the living room. I sat next to him on the sofa.

"Look, Max-"

"Shonna, we're going to make this as simple and as painless as possible. Okay?" he interrupted me. "Shonna, I love you, and I'm sorry I lied to you about my job. I've been selling drugs almost all of my life, but as you can see, unlike other people, I progressed in the game, and I've been doing very well for myself," he revealed.

"You...you love me?" I was at a loss for words.

"Yes, Shonna," he turned to fully face me.

"But, Max, we're not even in a relationship. We're just kicking it..."

"Yes, and that's your choice, not mine. If it were up to me, we'd be almost ready to move in together. Hell, the amount of time we've been friends, a lot of people get en-gaged and married in this length of time," he said. I just looked at him, frozen in shock. "Look, Shonna," he exhaled, "I'm not looking for you to say it back, and I know you just lost your husband and you're still healing from that. You've got this whole 'strong woman' thing going on, marching around like you don't need anybody and your whole life is one big secret," he said as he stared into my eyes, "but you need somebody. I could see your loneliness in your eyes the first time we met. I could smell your desire for companionship seeping from your pores as we sat there talking. I'm not saying that it has to be me, though I hope and pray that it will be me, but you're going to have to open up and let somebody in eventually."

"Max, I just don't know how to trust anymore," I admitted. "I always have my guard up because I don't know who I can trust."

"You can trust me. Haven't I proven that?"

"No, Max." I shook my head and frowned. "You're sitting here talking like I didn't just catch you in a whole lie. I thought I might have been able to trust you, but now I don't know anymore."

"You're one to talk though!" He was angry now, and possibly even offended. "I just caught you in the same lie!"

"No, Max. You don't understand-"

"Well, make me understand then, Shonna! Because I don't know how much clarification is necessary when you're talking about a drug transaction. It seems pretty clear to me!"

"Max, this ain't what I do! This ain't the life I live! I'm new to this shit! You want the truth? The whole truth?"

"Yes, Shonna, I do! Tell me the truth!"

"The truth is that my husband has been selling drugs for years behind my back, and I never knew. I was kidnapped, beaten, and tortured by men who killed my husband looking for his stash. When I broke free from them, I stole all of the weed, cocaine, and money they had and I've been trying to get rid of it. But then I found out Curtis left me a house, so I packed up and moved into the house, only to find tons of all kinds of shit in the damn house. So I've been trying to get rid of that shit too! This ain't what I do, Max. I've never done this before. I'm having to up a strap on niggas for trying to get over on me. I'm paranoid and suspicious; I'm carrying a pistol on me at all times. Hell, I had just pulled the gun on Darrel for making sudden movements right before you got there!"

"What in the entire fuck?!" I think I dropped too much on Max at one time because he was truly speechless. From the murder to the kidnapping to the drugs... Max had not known any of this before that moment. He just sat there staring at me with his mouth agape. He looked like I had just knocked him unconscious. When he came back to, he frowned at me and said, "You pulled a gun on Darrel?"

I got up. "You know what?" I turned to walk off, but he grabbed my hand. "All of that shit I just said, and all you heard was that I almost shot Darrel?"

"No, no! Shonna, I'm sorry. All of this has caught me off guard," he said as he jumped up and grabbed my other hand. "Did you say... damn," he said and dropped his head. "Shonna," he whispered.

"No, Max." I shook my head. "No." I knew what was about to happen before it even began.

"C'mere, Shonna." He sat back down on the sofa still holding my hands.

"Naw, Max. I'm good. I'm straight." I turned my head.

"C'mere, baby," he whispered as he tugged on my hands. Tears dropped from both of my eyes as I tried to hide my face.

"I'm good, Max."

"Shonna... are you crying?"

I turned and looked at him with my blurred vision. I could read the sadness and concern in his pupils as my pain lay exposed. I plopped down on the sofa next to him. Max had never seen me cry. I always kept my pain locked up tight until I was completely alone. He didn't even know how to react to my tears.

"Oh, baby," he whispered as he pulled me to him. "I'm so sorry. I'm so sorry, baby. I'm so sorry." He wrapped his arms around me and rocked back and forth as he kissed my forehead. "You didn't deserve that, baby. You didn't deserve any of that."

"It's my fault. I was so blind. All of those years, I trusted everything he ever told me, and all of it was a bunch of lies," I said between tears.

"It's not your fault," he whispered into my hair.

"Yes, it is. I trusted him too damn much like an idiot. If

you ever wondered why it's so hard for me to trust, why I'm so stand-offish, why I pull away and keep my distance, now you understand why. Right?"

"Hell yeah. I understand. How could I not?"

"It's nothing personal against you, Max. It's nothing you did wrong. It's my fucked up ass life. It's all the shit I've been through."

"I understand, baby, and it's not your fault. You're just trying to protect yourself from the same hurt you just escaped from," he said. "Hey, hey. Shonna, look at me." He lifted my chin with his thumb. "It's okay, Shonna. It's alright."

"Look at me," I said as I wiped away the tears. "Crying like a little weak ass bitch," I said as I tried to regain my composure. "I need to pull this shit together because these tears ain't gone help shit."

"You're human, Shonna. You have to let that shit out sometimes. Holding all of that in ain't gone do shit but drive you crazy," he told me. That shit went in one ear and out the other. I had snapped back.

"Hell naw," I told him. "I'm a boss ass bitch. I need to get myself together. This crying shit is for the birds."

"I'm going to run you a bath," he told me and then waited for my facial expression to change. "You need to relax. I'm going to run you a bubble bath and turn on the Jacuzzi jets in the tub. You just lay back and relax. Take a little time to clear your mind."

I watched him closely. He was hesitant and unsure with his offer- a result of my insistent rejection of these types of offers. His eyes kept looking off; he didn't want to look me in my eyes. He didn't want me to see his hurt when I rejected him again.

It's amazing what kind of effect a woman can have on a man. Maximillian had always struck me as an incredibly strong man, both physically and mentally. When we were at Pappadeux in Atlanta, I felt so safe with him. His presence demanded respect. His entire aura was that of an incredibly important, intelligent, well-respected man of stature. His self-confidence was high and he didn't seem to seek or need validation from anyone.

This was a different man I was looking at. This was a completely different side of Max. To see him so unsure of himself, as if he was worried that he wasn't good enough or just wasn't enough period…I could've slapped myself. This man cared about me and had even admitted that he loved me. He had let me in so much deeper than I had ever allowed him to delve. I felt like shit. I had pushed this man away so much that he had started doubting himself. That's not how you treat someone you care about, and I couldn't deny that I cared about him. Look at how much time I had been spending with him. Even if he wasn't my boyfriend, at that moment he was the only friend I had that I was even speaking to. He was the most consistent person in my life, and I really had been mis-treating him.

"Naw, I got it," I said to him and watched the relief spread across his face. He just sat there for a second as I head-ed toward the bedroom.

"I- I can run it for you, baby. It's no problem. You need some time to just relax," he said.

"No, baby. I'm good. You've done enough." With that, I went down the hallway to his bedroom and turned on the water in the tub. I grabbed my bag from the chaise lounge in his bedroom and added the bubble bath to the water.

I sat there and watched the water run as I let my mind wander. I remembered the first time I took a shower after I escaped from the warehouse. When I turned the water on, I just stood there and watched it. I had found a whole new appreciation for hot, clean running water. Max had no idea what I had gone through in that warehouse. I had come out a completely different person, and yet, I could still see remnants of the old me in myself. I could act like I gave no fucks, but the truth was that I still had a little piece of my heart left. It had become evident that I may have needed to just attempt to turn that little crumb over to Max.

I knew Max was going to sit next to the tub while I was soaking, so I prepared myself for it mentally. Outside of everything we had omitted, our communication skills were on point. We could talk anywhere about anything and we almost always saw eye-to-eye on everything. I knew what I was risking losing at the moment I decided to withhold information from Max, but I also was aware of the risks I would run by telling him the whole truth.

I had already had a bath a few hours ago, so I was really just trying to relax. I set the jets and leaned back and closed my eyes. As I heard Max's feet approaching, I steadied my breathing and calmed my nerves. When I opened my eyes,

Max was standing over me with a glass of red wine in both hands. I gave him a slight smile and took one of the glasses from him.

He hopped on top of the sink and just sat there. He wasn't looking at me or anything in particular. He was lost in his own thoughts and drinking like he was trying to find answers to his questions in the bottom of his glass.

"Shonna, I love you," he said out the blue without even lifting his head. "It's hard as hell for me to admit because I know you don't feel the same way. I can't make you love me, but I'm not going to treat you any differently just because you don't."

"Max, stop."

"No, listen to me, Shonna. You can't live your life never trusting anyone, always alone, keeping people at arm's length. As complete of a woman as you believe yourself to be, you still are going to need somebody. You already admitted you know next to nothing about the shit you're doing. The least you can do is let me help you. Do yourself that favor. Hell, do me that one favor so I don't lose my sanity worrying about you. This shit is dangerous, Shonna. Especially for a woman. Even more so for a woman who doesn't know what the fuck she's doing. We don't have to be in a relationship, but we should at least be in a partnership."

"Max, would you just stop and hear me out for a second?" I asked quietly. He nodded for me to continue. "I think that maybe we should give it a chance. I mean, we're damn near doing everything people do when they're in a relationship anyway. We're calling each other all the time. I'm always over your house. We're having sex, hanging out, telling each other our deepest secrets. The only thing we're not doing is going out and being seen in public," I told him.

"That's what I've been trying to explain to you." He threw his hands up. "You're acting like you just had some kind of epiphany, when I've been telling you this for months now."

"It's not so much of an epiphany as an acceptance of the true circumstances of the situation. I've just come to realize that I'm going to need somebody and I've already established a relationship with you, so I might as well build with you from here."

"So you're settling because I'm convenient?" he huffed as he crossed his arms, getting offended.

"Settling? Who said I was settling? You need to stop being so defensive, Max. I'm not settling with you. You're a great guy. Don't you see that? All I'm saying is that I see it myself now. We're great together. We're damn near best friends. I'm saying let's do this. Let's be great together. We can turn this city upside-down."

Max just stared at me for a moment. I could see the gears turning in his mind. He was formulating something, but I couldn't really tell what.

"So we're together now?" he asked my closed eyes.

"Yeah," I nodded and sighed.

"Okay," I heard him say, followed by silence. I opened one eye to find Max was no longer in the room.

Chapter 12

When I got out of the tub, I lotioned up and slipped on the lingerie I had just purchased. It was a simple black push up bra, black lace-trimmed fish net panties that laced up the back, and black fish net stockings that laced up the back of the legs. I examined myself in the mirror as I sprayed a mist of Moon Light Path scented diamond dust body mist from Bath & Body Works over my breasts, chest, and neck. My hair and make-up were just as flawless as my curves. I loved everything about myself, even the evil I saw swimming in my own pupils.

Opening the bathroom door, I realized that the lights were off in the bedroom. There were lit candles all over the bedroom and rose petals on the bed and the floor. Maxwell's "Ascension" was playing softly from the stereo. Max was lying across white silk sheets wearing red silk boxers and holding two flutes of champagne. He looked so corny, I busted into laughter. He had what I thought was his "come fuck me" look going on, which was sexy enough by itself, but the red silk boxers were just too much. I couldn't even hold in my giggles. He was just too hot for me.

"What's funny?" he asked as he offered me a flute of champagne.

"You," I could barely get the one word out without choking on my own laughter. "You're so corny. Look at you."

"What" he chuckled innocently as he looked himself over.

"Bruh, you got on red silk boxers. Really, fool? You're so crazy."

"You don't like them? I'm not sexy in them?"

"You look sexy in anything, baby. It's just very cliché. That's all."

"Well, come and be cliché with me then, sexy," he said as he offered me a hand and helped me onto the bed. "C'mere, baby," he whispered as I slid next to him. I took the champagne and turned up the flute as he lay next to me on his side undressing what little bit I was wearing with his eyes.

"I love this," I said as I sipped. "This is really good."

"Only the best for my baby," he said as he tossed back the last of his own glass and kissed my cheek. "What's this you got on, baby?"

"A little something I put together just for you."

"Do you feel like modeling it for me? Stand up and let me see you, beautiful."

I closed my eyes as I stood up and allowed his last word to sink in. "Beautiful." I should've had a lot more confidence in myself than I did. I had always been so unsure of myself, always wondered what men saw in me. In my eyes, I was just me, plain ole me. Sometimes I brushed my hair and sometimes I didn't. I hardly ever wore any type of make-up, and before I had discovered Jimmy Choos, none of my heels were name brand or even worn more than a couple of times.

I had discovered an entirely different dimension I could travel to mentally to become a brand new person. She was my alter-ego. A bad bitch with hella confidence that took no bullshit, she was everything I had never been. She had an inferno blazing in her eyes and a blizzard blowing through her veins, and I promise you, if pushed too far, she'd blow out a nigga's brains. She was not one to be fucked with.

I closed my eyes as me and opened them as her and runway walked through Maximillian's bedroom like I had modeled in Paris or New York during Fashion Week. When I turned around, I looked back at Max and winked. Max sat up in the bed with his jaw agape. His eyes were as big as half dollar coins. By the time I made it back across the room, Max was up on his knees studying me intently.

"Shonna," he whispered awestruck. "Shonna, Shonna, Shonna," he whispered again and again. I heard nothing. I had zoned out, and Prince's "The Most Beautiful Girl in the World" had me going. "Slim!" he shouted, and I snapped out of it.

"Huh?" I stopped in my tracks.

"What the hellllllll…" he said. "What just happened? You zoned the fuck out."

"I… ummm… I don't know. I guess I was just feeling the song," I chuckled uneasily, blushing slightly. Honestly, I couldn't even remember what I had just been doing.

"I guess so," Max mumbled, but there was something glistening in his eyes, something he looked off in an attempt to hide.

I walked over to the bed, bent over with my palms flat on the pillow top mattress, and pressed my lips against his. I waited exactly seven seconds before Max exhaled and kissed me back. I know because I counted. When he did, the passion was so intense it made every worry I had feel obsolete. He pulled me onto the bed with him and laid me down, and everything in me just surrendered to him.

His arms engulfed my body, allowing his warmth to calm me even more. Holding me tight, he kissed me over and over, as if he had an insatiable appetite for my lips. It felt like he hadn't given any thought to having sex with me. All he wanted to do was love me and love on me. He was more than satisfied just holding me, caressing me, and kissing me. Making love would have just been the bonus round in his game show because he had already won his prize.

My hand held the back of his neck, urging him on as his fingers ran up my thigh and then slid beneath me to caress my lower back. I melted into the sheets. I felt so beautiful, so desirable, so loved... something that I hadn't felt in years. Max removed my bra and my body screamed "yes" as he took the sweet flesh of my left areola between his lips. He slid my panties to the side and I gushed as his fingers gently caressed and then entered my wetness. My eyes closed and my head rolled back as he moaned for me, as if he could feel my sensations as well.

As I opened my eyes, I glanced into his. He was in love with me. I could see it written there in his eyes as if it were a beautiful poem on a piece of stationery. All he really wanted was for me to read that poem and interpret it the way he had written it. At that moment, I finally got the message.

He lifted himself and slid down between my legs. The lace slid over my hips, down my thighs and legs, and landed on the floor. My legs spread. My lungs inhaled. My fingers gripped the sheets. I couldn't scream or moan; I was speechless. With every firework, my heart somersaulted. With every sensation, my soul cartwheeled.

My breathing grew heavier as the fire rose from my toe nails and shot straight through me to the very ends of my hair. My back arched involuntarily as my hands let go of the sheets and ran my fingers over his waves. He looked up into my eyes just as I was looking down at him and our eyes connected. Something inside of me felt locked into place, as if we had suddenly synced. He read me and my emotions. He could see the pleasure as if it were pouring from my retinas. He looked so calm, so at peace, as if he was enjoying what he was doing to me.

"Baby," I whispered while still staring into his eyes. That one word seemed to motivate him even more and I felt him dive deeper. I must have lost my mind. I screamed his name and my eyes closed tight. My fingers gripped the sheets so tight one of my nails bent back. I didn't feel it, nor did I care. An entire flood came flowing onto the sheets, and I struggled to catch my breath.

Max kissed his way up my stomach, but once my breathing steadied, I ambushed him with kisses. I wrapped myself around him and refused to let go. He was the water to my drought, and I was trying to get wet. Before I even knew what I was doing, I had ripped the corny ass silk boxers right off his ass and had flipped him over on the bed. He looked at me in shock.

"Lay back," I told him, "and spread your legs some." He did just as I instructed and I crawled up the bed between his legs. He looked down at me as I wrapped my hand around his dick and stroked it. It was hard enough to break ice- pun intended.

All of this time he had been putting it down on me. I mean he had been seriously putting in work. All of this hollering and screaming he had me doing, that was not something I usually did. Having me climbing the walls, gripping the sheets, and screaming his name, that was unheard of. All of these multiple orgasms he was causing me to have over and over, back to back, he had accomplished the impossible. There was no way I was about to continue to keep allowing him to drive me crazy and I not show up and show out on his ass as well. He was a beast in the bed, but it takes a beast to tame a beast.

I had learned long ago that there really was a technique to sucking dick. I would always see my friends posting questions about whether big girls or skinny girls, black girls or white girls, ghetto girls or "boujee" girls sucked dick better. The truth was that none of those things were even a factor. I was a firm believer that the best head came from a woman who actually gave a fuck about what she was doing. It's all about a woman's attitude. If you don't feel like sucking dick, then you just need to tell him that shit because if you do it anyway, your whole demeanor will say "Fuck you, your dick, and this blow job, nigga."

A woman's entire thought process and purpose while she has a dick in her mouth should be to take that man to a high greater than or equal to that of her pussy. The entire purpose of the act is to pleasure the man, so the woman has to truly care about the man's pleasure to put effort into taking him there. You have to be serious about what you're doing, like you mean it, and keep the ultimate goal in mind. When you didn't come to play, it shows. Your one and only goal in the entire production is to take this nigga's soul. If you keep that in mind, his entire experience will be ten times better.

My only experience with giving head was with Curtis, but he taught me everything he could and everything else I learned from PornHub and X Videos. My performance this particular night with Max, though, made me realize that I had something special. I was one in a million.

As I stroked Max's dick, I thought about how I actually felt about him. Then I thought about what he had just done to me and what he had done to me every time we had made love. I had something to prove. I took one last look in his eyes and then wrapped my tongue around the head of his dick. I swirled my tongue around it and then flicked it on the tip. Then I put the whole thing in my mouth as far as it would go. I had long ago mastered breathing through my nose. Up and down, in and out, twisting and swirling. I glanced up and saw him watching me. His head went back as he grunted, "Oh shit." I had him. I shoved his dick into the back of my throat and opened my mouth wide. Then I ran it in and out of my throat over and over and then suddenly closed my jaws around it tight and sucked it fast. His fingers ran through my hair and then pushed my head down on his dick, forcing it deep into my throat until he exploded against my tonsils.

I came up off of it and loosened my grip on it as Max attempted to regain his composure. I looked at his closed eyes and clenched jaw and made that split second decision that always changes the nature of a relationship. I wrapped my lips back around his dick and listened as he inhaled sharply. His reflexes kicked in and he attempted to push my head back, something I had been fully expecting. I tightened my grip again, locked my neck, and pulled back on the head of his dick with my jaws sucked in so tight my teeth almost cut into them.

He was there and I knew it. Nothing was impossible to me, especially when I was this determined. I ran his dick deep into my throat, and Max released a high-pitched scream and another load down my throat. That was it. Mission accomplished. I took his soul.

There was nothing after that. When you do that to a man, you'd better make sure you get yours beforehand because when you take a man's soul, it literally drains him of all of his energy. Max fell into a sleep so deep, he could have been considered unconscious. I blew out the two dozen candles he had scattered throughout the room and snuggled beneath him. As comatose as he was, Max wrapped himself around me and held me tight. For the first time in forever, because of that one subconscious notion, I felt loved, cherished, and desired.

Chapter 13

Max and I didn't waste any time. He wanted to know exactly what I was trying to get rid of, so four days later, I met up with him and took him to my house. He was my first house guest. When I took him down into the Drug Lair, he almost lost his mind.

"Shonna! Oh my fucking God!" If his words didn't say enough, his facial expression said it all. "This is what the fuck you're trying to get rid of? And you're selling the shit to folks like Darrel? It'll take you forever to get rid of all of this shit like that!"

"Well, I have a couple of larger clients that buy more in bulk," I explained.

"Yeah, but you have a lot of weed down here, and even though it's packaged pretty air tight and it takes a while to go bad, you still don't want to hold it too long because it's still very perishable."

"Well, I'm no expert at this shit. I've been learning as I go. So are you going to help me get rid of this shit or nah?" I asked him with my hands in the pockets of my Saint Laurent jeans.

"I mean, I really don't have a choice. You've got shelves of felonies and whole jars full of fed charges down here. Plus, Shonna, this ain't no business for you. You shouldn't be involved in this shit. Look at you. You look like you need to be married to a lawyer or a judge somewhere with your feet propped up in Chanel sandals on a cherrywood desk in his mansion. You're not a drug dealer, Shonna. This is not the life for you."

"I've been doing damn good up until this point," I told him. "I've gotten rid of more than half of the shit I had. I don't have time for your opinions and commentary, Max," I huffed. "Either you're going to help or you're not, but if you are, I'd appreciate more work and less discussion."

"Don't be trying to act all hard and shit. I'm going to help you. Let me make a few phone calls to line some shit up and see what's up. In the meantime, I got some other business to discuss with you."

"Well, what's up? I'm all ears," I said as I folded my arms across my chest and leaned against the table.

"Ummm… you got somewhere we can sit down and talk?"

"Yeah, c'mon. We can sit in the living room," I said as I led him back up the stairs. "And don't be looking at my ass," I giggled as I looked back at him.

"I can't help it," he chuckled. "That ass does some amazing things."

"Whatever. C'mon. The living room is through here."

"You have a beautiful house," he said as he looked around in awe.

"Thank you. I kept it just the way Curtis left it to me. All of the furniture, curtains, and décor came with the house. I just moved in with my clothes."

"He had really great taste. It's a brand new house, too. He probably had it custom built."

"He did. I have all of the paperwork for it," I said as I sat down on the sofa and turned on the TV. "Have a seat," I told Max. He sat next to me and twiddled his thumbs a bit. "What's up, baby?" I interrupted his nervousness.

"This shit you're doing- selling drugs and shit- this ain't you, baby. I mean, if you've gotten rid of as much of it as you say you have, you've been doing a damn good job, but I think you should leave that shit to me. Let me get rid of the rest of that shit for you. I've got something more suitable for you," he told me.

"Something more suitable? Like what?"

"I've got this scheme. My homeboys have been pulling this move with their hoes and shit, but the shit ain't been going right because they don't give a fuck about the bitches because they're hoes. I want us to try it and see if we can pull it off," he told me. I just looked at him. Just the fact that he had said all of that and hadn't ran me the scenario told me he didn't think I'd go for it.

"So what's the scheme, Max?"

"Fridays are paydays generally speaking. Everybody is cashing their checks and shit after work. Mexicans cash their checks at places like gas stations and liquor stores because most of them are illegal and don't have ID's to get a bank account. They also have a lot of money on them. You follow me so far?"

"Yeah, so far."

"So we're going to sit you up in a liquor store or gas station in these areas where there are a whole lot of Mexicans. You go in the store, you buy something, and while you're in line or checking out, you flirt with one of the guys and give him your number, give him a room number at a hotel. You meet up with him at the hotel to fuck him for a decent fee. You get him in the room, get him undressed, and then I pop out of the bathroom with my forty and stick him up."

He didn't look at me the entire time he was talking. He seemed to be talking to his feet. I could tell he had serious doubts about whether I'd be down with the move and he was probably even afraid that I was going to snap at him.

"So you think it's going to work?" I asked him.

"Yeah. It's fa sho money, and you know they make plenty of money."

"It sounds dangerous though."

"Well, you know I ain't gone let shit happen to you. I love you, baby. We're going to take every precaution we can to make sure you're completely safe. We can practice and do test runs so you can see what it feels like to actually be in the situation and you'll know how to handle the different ways it could go." He looked at me to be sure I was following him. "I want you to understand, Shonna," he said as he turned to me and took both of my hands in his own, "this shit can be very, very dangerous…"

"Man, Max, if you don't get the fuck out of here with that mushy sentimental shit," I said as I snatched my hands from him. "This is business. Do you want to do this shit or not?"

"Yeah," he was taken aback by my attitude. "But I'm just trying to warn you about the dangers in this shit before you jump into it head first."

"You sound more like you're trying to scare me out of doing the shit," I frowned. "Look, if we're going to do this relationship and business shit, you're going to have to learn how to separate the two. You brought this shit o tome because you know I'm the woman for the job. If you didn't think I was capable, you would've propositioned the next bitch with it, so miss me with the violin and the black and white floor model TV ass shit."

"What the fuck?" Max looked at me like I had grown two more heads.

"What, nigga?"

"Who the fuck are you and what the fuck did you do with my baby?"

"Mane, Max-"

"Mane? Shonna, what the hell has gotten into you?"

"Max if you don't gone on somewhere with that bull-shit!"

"What the fuck are you talking about? You don't talk like this. How did you just jump gangsta on me all of a sudden?" Max was sincerely in shock.

"I didn't jump gangsta. I'm being straight forward about the situation. If we're going to do this shit, then we can go ahead and get to work. I don't know why you're always trying to be so damn gentle and sentimental with me. I see I'm going to have to show you some shit," I told him.

"It's not about me being gentle or sentimental. You're a woman. I have to approach you a certain way," he tried to explain, but of course, I wasn't hearing it.

"Woman or not, nigga, I'm grown as hell. The only thing you have to do is keep it a hundred with me and I'm good. Don't be trying to sugar coat shit, ole Willie Wonka ass nigga," I said and rolled my eyes at him.

"Aye, you ain't gone be talking crazy to me," he tried to puff his chest out.

"You better quit trying to pump your nuts up at me before I let some air out of them mother fuckers for you, Max. I don't know what the fuck you think this is, but it ain't that."

"Shonna, have you lost your damn mind? Why the fuck are you- you know what? I'm just going to leave. I ain't with this shit. You're getting disrespectful as hell for no damn reason."

"I wouldn't be disrespectful if you weren't treating me like a damn child. You act like I can't handle myself. What the fuck do you think I was doing before you came along? I've been handling my own business ever since my husband has been gone, so don't come up in here acting like I fucking need you or like I can't get with the shit because I promise I'll have your head spinning how fast I prove you wrong."

"So that's what it is? You don't need me, and I know it, Shonna. I'm not in denial about that shit. You're a strong independent woman. That's one thing that attracted me to you. I never said you needed me. I did, however, think that you wanted me. Now, I'm not so sure," he said with a look of disappointment slathered across his face like mashed potatoes in a food fight. "I think I'm just going to go," he said as he rose to his feet.

"You finna go?" I looked at him in disgust.

"Yeah, I'm finna go," he said as he started towards the kitchen.

"So that's all it takes for you to walk out on me?" I got up and followed behind him.

"I'm not about to sit here and let you talk to me out the side of your neck. I love you, Shonna, but I'm a man before anything."

"Nobody said you weren't a man. All I asked was that

you come correct when you bring something to me and stop acting like I'm a sheet of glass."

"I came at you," he said as he spun around, "the way a man is supposed to come at a woman he loves- with respect, consideration, and concern. I'm not about to bring this serious ass shit to you like you're a bitch off the street. I'm going to make sure you understand how dangerous this shit is and that I got you a hundred percent the entire time," he said as he punched the palm of his hand for emphasis.

"That shit doesn't have to be said, Max! It's understood. You've been begging me to trust you and give you a chance for a while now. Why would I think you wouldn't have my back?"

"You're so fucking doubtful about every damn thing. Why wouldn't I try to reassure you? I've had to reassure you about everything else we've done so far. Every bit of progress we've made has been a result of me persuading and coercing you into trusting me. So why would I even begin to think that anything was going to come with cooperation or compliance from you without some sort of debate or struggle?"

"So that's what it is, huh?" I scoffed. "You're so used to everything just falling into your lap- including bitches- that you can't put in a bit of work for something you claim you really want."

"Shonna, that's not what-"

"No, Max. You can save the dissertation," I said quietly. I was a bit too calm even for my own comfort. "Let me explain something to you. We can be together. We can fall in love. We can Bonnie and Clyde, ride or die this shit out. But you want to be my one and only so bad that you've forgotten that you aren't the only man who wants me. Hell, even some of these women be out here trying to holler at me. I look good and I know it. These Jimmy Choos and these Red Bottoms raise eyebrows and turn heads. You're not my last resort, but you're certainly not my only option. I'm not about to just give you a damn thing. If you want me, you have to show it, prove it, work for it. This shit just ain't that easy."

"It's hard to find someone real these days, Shonna. You've got somebody who truly loves you. I try to hold tight to everything we have. You're special to me," he told me.

"All you have to do is keep it a hundred and you'll get my respect. This shit ain't about the sex or nothing you buy me. I work hard for my paper, so you're going to have to work for my time and my love. Yes, you had to persuade and coerce me. You had to show and prove. I don't trust people. I handle my own business and stay to myself. So for me to let you inside in any way, it was going to take some work anyway. I'm not going to settle for just any man. Ninety-nine percent of men don't deserve me or a woman like me and don't know how to handle or treat the type of woman I am. I cater to my man. I cook, clean, iron, anything needed for the man in my life. I have to choose a man carefully so that my big ass heart doesn't get abused because believe me, mother fuckers will abuse the shit out of a bitch with a big ass heart who cares too damn much. I'm spontaneous and fun-loving. I set it off in the car and play-fight in the living room. I help fix on the car, move and put together furniture, do my own do-it-yourself projects, and decorate the house. How many females do you know that will get under the hood of a car? Get oil and grease under their manicure? Know that the drill bits come separate from the drill? Know how to find studs in a wall without a stud finder? Will risk breaking a nail lifting a sofa?" I paused for effect. "Not many. Exactly. I used to work at a warehouse and now I sell a felonious amount of drugs for a living. Of course I was hesitant about allowing any man, not just you, even close to me. On top of being the perfect, ideal woman, I'm also the most imperfect, most dangerous woman as well. If you want me, I come with a whole lot of work. Ain't none of this about to just fall into your lap."

Max turned around to face me squarely and looked me straight in my eyes. We stood there in a stare-off for about three solid minutes. I could tell he was searching for something in the depths of my eyes, but he was seeking an answer within himself as well. Just as I was growing tired of the awkward silence and felt like my eyes were going to chap and crack from lack of moisture, Max grabbed my chin and kissed me so deeply, he literally had to catch me. My legs gave out beneath me and my head felt light.

When we pulled away, our eyes connected again for about five seconds and then we attacked each other. Clothes flew across the room, fluttering like doves released after a wedding. We tumbled onto the sofa, and I found myself straddling him, my tongue touching his tonsils, my hips already rolling in anticipation. Max's lips pulled away from our kiss to engulf my right nipple as his right hand palmed my left breast. I sighed as he suckled like a baby. My head rolled back and he kissed up my breastbone, up my neck, and playfully bit my chin.

I lifted up and felt him rub his hardness back and forth in my dripping juices. As I slid down on his rod, the sensation shot through my entire body. Max and I both sighed in relief. I closed my eyes as I bounced on it and rode Max like there was no tomorrow. My curls fell into my face and I pushed them behind me and then leaned down and kissed my man. His fingers gripped my hips, pulling me back down each time. I came up on it.

I zoned out. Everything about it felt so good, so right. And yet, something deep inside of me still felt so wrong. But that something I had come to learn to ignore. Time seemed to slow down as I enjoyed each stroke, relished in the pleasure of Max being deep inside of me, feeling like I was moving in slow motion. My moans grew louder as the sensations grew stronger.

Suddenly, Max gripped my waist tighter, stood up with my legs around his waist, and then pinned me against the wall. I wrapped my arms around his neck and closed my eyes as our lips met again and he pumped deep into me slowly. This man didn't just love me. He desired me. It felt like he wanted to devour…consume me.

He carried me out of the living room and into the kitchen and sat me down on the island's marble countertop. I hollered out as he dug deep, screamed as he hit it hard.

"Oh, God, Max! Fuck me!" I screamed out as he gripped my ass and drilled me.

"I'm done playing with you, Shonna," he said through gritted teeth. "Either you gone be mine or I'm gone quit fucking with you."

"Max, Max!" He was tearing my pussy up. I couldn't even begin to comprehend what he was saying to me, but somehow 'quit fucking with you' registered.

"Tell me it's mine," he demanded.

"What?"

"Say it's my pussy. Tell me it's mine," he said again. I was sure I was going to be bow legged from him being dick-deep in my stomach.

"It's yours, baby!" I yelled. "It's all yours!"

"So you gone stop acting so hard and act right?"

"Huh?" What was with the questions? Damn! Can a bitch just fuck and nut?

"Say you gone get some act right!" he said as he smacked my ass.

"I am, baby! Shit! Shit! I am!"

I saw his eyes roll back just as mine detoured to the back of my head as well.

"Fuck!" I heard him yell out just as I felt my entire body become overcome with fire and then shake uncontrollably. My back arched and I screamed out... and then Max shot nut so deep in my womb I felt the heat from it against my stomach.

He kept my ass in his grip as he lay on my breasts recuperating and trying to catch his breath. He stood up and put my legs down and walked back into the living room. I sat up on the counter just in time to see him come back out fully dressed and buckling his belt.

"Max…where are you going?" I frowned as I asked him, confused about what the hell just happened here.

"I'll be back tomorrow to get this shit out of here," he said over his shoulder without even looking at me and then he left before I could get even one more word out.

Chapter 14

From that moment on, everything changed. Max and I hit the game hard. We were in go mode and there was no stopping us. Monday through Thursday, Max and I handled mad business getting rid of all of the drugs I had in the Drug Lair, plus all of Max's regular business. Business had picked up some for Darrell too, so he was calling twice a week for more product, while I was still dealing with Big Bang and Max still had his regular customers as well.

Friday, Saturday, and Sunday, though... Max and I were all about the move. Max and his friend Montrell had staged a few practice scenarios for me so I would know what to expect, but by the third practice it was clear I was a natural at it. So Montrell disappeared back to wherever Max had gotten him from, and Max and I set up dates.

In the beginning, Max and I agreed to only do about three dates a night. They were always in three different parts of the city and they were always spaced out to accommodate anything that could possibly cause us to take a few extra minutes getting rid of one of the guys.

We were all about the in and out. I'd get the guy in the room, get him comfortable, get him out of his shirt and almost always out of his pants, give Max the code, and then we would jack his ass. Three dates a night, anywhere from nine hundred dollars up to about thirty-five hundred per lick, three nights a week. We always cut at least ten racks over a weekend, and we split it all straight down the middle.

I didn't know what Max was doing with his cut, and I didn't care. He didn't know anything about my safe deposit boxes, and I never intended to tell him. All I knew was that I was all for stacking my money. I added it to the pot. The money I was making from getting rid of the drugs was enough to take care of anything I needed and allowed me to go shopping whenever I wanted. Outside of seeing Max during our weekend hold-ups, I only saw him when he came by to pick up product or when we occasionally hung out and fucked, which was about once a week.

Max and his whereabouts were not what I was on, and I know deep down inside he knew that. That was my first mistake. I'd be all lovey-dovey and googly-eyed when we did have our quality time, but when he left, I was straight back to business. Part of our alone time was fake for me too. Sure, I enjoyed his company and having someone to feel me up every once in a while, but occasionally I caught myself wishing he would just fuck the shit out of me and bounce. I mean, I wasn't in denial about the sex. I knew one thing for sure: I was a grown ass woman and was going to have to get my dick from somewhere. I made sure I rode the shit out of Max's dick every time we linked up to make sure it would hold me over until the next week. The reality was that I didn't have to have all of that love shit, though. I gave it to him to appease him, and in return, he fucked me cross-eyed. I guess you have to give some to get some.

In between all of this, I was still hitting the skies to get around to collect from all of the safe deposit boxes Curtis had all over the country. I was never gone more than three days and Max was never the wiser to any of it, but, boy, if he had checked my closets at my house, he'd have known that more than half of the shit I owned wasn't even available in Memphis. I went shopping in every city I visited and spent sometimes hundreds of thousands of dollars. And every single city I visited was commemorated with a pair of Jimmy Choos that I hadn't seen anywhere else.

A few months went by with that flow, and Max and I had settled into a routine. We both started to get bored and decided to raise the number of dates on the weekend. We went from three a night to five, and then seven. Max even told me to accept dates with black men and white men too. Truck drivers, dope boys, we didn't care. We got up to nine dates a night. We'd do one every hour starting at eight and we'd be home by six. The problem was that we were running out of motels and hotels to pull the move at. We were treading on dangerous ground using the same motel more than once a month. We had even been careful to only do one date per night in each of the nine precincts in the city. That way, if the police were called out by one of our dumb ass victims and they put out a broadcast, it was unlikely they'd be looking for us across town. We had even been careful to rotate out our fake ID's when we paid for the rooms. There was no such thing as getting caught. Those words weren't even in our vocabulary.

What was in my vocabulary was "bored" and "sexually frustrated." Max had me fucked up. I had been feeling my body changing. My sex drive had heightened and I had tried to explain that to Max, but he wasn't hearing it. I had even tried to get him to come through a few times other than our normal days, but he always had business to handle. He had done all of the whining and crying about how bad he wanted me and wasn't even doing what he needed to do to keep me. I talked to and flirted with men all day every day to set up these dates. Some of them were talking a good game too. Some of them had money- real money- and offered to take me on trips overseas and buy me cars and jewelry. They complained about how hard it was to find a real woman who was beautiful, smart, and mature. Meanwhile, I couldn't get Max to pay me much more attention sexually than our usual weekly appointment.

I got tired of that shit. I got tired of being horny and feeling like Max had gotten over on me. I could have found myself a man who was going to actually be around and fuck me when I needed to be fucked if I had known that Max was going to act like I was on his schedule all the time. I kept telling myself the relationship was supposed to be give and take, not all about him and what he had going on, even though what was left of my heart kept telling me to be patient with him. I had learned long ago that my heart would get me fucked off if I listened only to it and not to common sense, reason, and intuition as well.

My relationship with Max had lost its spark. There was no spontaneity. We had sex on a schedule. We hardly held much of a conversation when we were around each other. I don't know what was going through Max's head, but he had to have been a damn fool to think that I wasn't going to notice the sudden complete change in everything that was us.

I sat up one night thinking and drinking. I had let the hard alcohol go, but I was still holding on to my wine. I had called Max earlier in the afternoon to see if he would come by after he finished his rounds and hang out with me for a while. His only response was "I'll see" and I hadn't heard from him since. It was ten o' clock at night and Max had yet to call me back. I was fed up, so I decided to do something about it.

I knew Max would be looking for the Range Rover and it would be hard to hide from him if I drove it because of its size, so I hopped in the Audi. My first mind told me to go by his house. I had never shown up at his house uninvited even though Max had given me a key to his house months before. My second mind told me to drive through the neighborhoods where I knew he always hung out. A wise woman once told me to always go with my first mind, though, so I went to Max's house.

I didn't pull in the driveway. Instead I parked across the street two houses down and just sat there looking at Max's car parked in his driveway, unsure what I should even think. I had only been sitting there for seven minutes before Max came out of the house wearing tan slacks and a blue button down, hopped into his car, and pulled off. I followed him at a safe distance as he drove from his cute little quiet neighborhood in Cordova to the Hickory Hill area and pulled into an apartment complex behind Hickory Ridge Mall.

Part of me was still giving him the benefit of the doubt, but the other half of me just knew better. I watched as he sat in the car and called someone on his cell, and then a woman who was half naked came out and hopped into his passenger seat and he pulled off again. That one moment said so much to me without words even being spoken. He didn't care about this bitch at all. He didn't get out to knock on her door; he called her to come out. He had never done me like that. He didn't open the door for her; he always opened the car door for me. He obviously didn't even care that she was half dressed because she had on a Pepto-Bismol colored tube top and a blue jean skirt that barely existed and her ass cheeks were hanging from underneath.

Still, he had me fucked up. I followed them at a distance as he drove down Knight Arnold Road and made a right on Lamar. Lamar? I frowned as I continued to follow from three cars behind them. Max pulled into the parking lot of a run-down hotel at the corner of Lamar and American Way and parked and the two of them got out and went inside. The hotel used to be nice back in its day; it was once a Ramada. But those days were long gone, and now it was mostly frequented by prostitutes who worked the different corners up and down Lamar and the lot lizards who slithered across the street from the truck stop.

I went into the building and rounded the corner at the elevators in time to see them get into one. I stood there and waited for the elevator to stop on a floor. Three. They were on the third floor. I got into the next elevator and made it to the third floor just in time to see Max's hand pressed against the small of her bare back, ushering her into the room.

I could've snapped at that moment. I could've gone crazy, lost my mind. I could've gone banging on the door and fucked that bitch up when they opened the door. But all I really wanted to do was make sure I wasn't making any assumptions. I stood there by the elevators for about five minutes. I wasn't worried about the staff watching the security cameras or security walking down the hall. The building was in such bad condition, I was sure the cameras were inoperable and security was probably asleep in their little truck in the parking lot.

I walked down the hall to the door of the room I had seen them go into. Room three twenty-three. I shook my head at how fucked up the situation was. I wanted to turn and run away, get back into my car, go home, and go to bed. I wanted to act like I hadn't seen any of this. But a voice deep down inside told me to stop running and face the truth.

I pressed my ear to the door and could hear her moaning quietly. I felt heat rise from my toes and creep slowly up into my earlobes. My breath felt hotter each time I exhaled. I felt steam pouring out of my ears and my heart felt like it was about to pound out of my chest. I stood there listening to her moans as they grew louder and turned into impassioned screams. I could hear everything. His hand smacking her ass, flesh smacking against flesh, the raggedy bed as it creaked under the weight of their movement, his rapid heavy breathing. And each sound was accompanied by the visual my mind conjured to match.

She probably hadn't even gotten out of her tube top and her skirt was probably up around her waist. He hadn't taken the time to knock on her door for her to come out, so I knew he hadn't even cared enough to undress her. I told myself he didn't love her; he loved me. I convinced myself that she didn't mean anything to him. She was just a fuck, and it was I who he desired. I promised myself that there was no one in the world who could take my place in any man's life and that she must have benefitted Max in some type of way. And yet, as much as I stood there and pep-talked myself, the sounds from the other side of the door told the story. As much of a woman as I knew I was, my heart was crushed. I had trusted him. I had let him in. He was the only person I had trusted since Curtis had been ripped away from me, and he had betrayed me.

I heard Max's unmistakable grunt and the bed creaked louder and faster. The woman's screams sounded as though whatever Max was doing to her hurt more than it felt good. He wasn't just having sex with her; he was fucking her. He was fucking her the way I wanted him to fuck me. Royally. Relentlessly. He was always so gentle with me, so loving and caring, even when what I really wanted was sex so nasty and so rough that there would be no doubt I was going to hell. But here he was fucking this mud duck's lace front sideways, even though she was so much less than I was and she obviously couldn't even take dick. As bad as I wanted Max to dislocate my hip and realign the vertebrae in my spine, and here he was digging out this rookie- ass bitch's guts. I could've slapped the shit out of his dumb ass.

My feet were planted at the door, tears forming in the corners of my eyes. I was hurt, but I was more angry than anything else. She was loud. I had moved my ear off of the door and could still hear her clearly. He wasn't even breaking me off proper and had the nerve to be fucking someone else. He claimed to love me, but was giving my dick to this nothing ass tramp. I just shook my head. He didn't even know what I was capable of and I knew I could hurt him worse than he could ever hurt me.

The woman started screaming, crying out, telling Max how bad it hurt, begging him to wait, stop. There was no change in the creaking of the bed. He didn't give a fuck.

"Take this dick, bitch," I heard him growl.

"No, no! Milli! I can't! I can't, Milli! I can't! It hurts!" I heard her cry out. Milli? I frowned in amusement. Was that his street name? I almost burst into a fit of laughter right there at the door while I was eavesdropping.

"Shut the fuck up and take this dick, bitch! Stop running," he ordered. She quieted down, but I could still hear her whimpering. "Talking all that shit about what you gone do. You was talking like you was big and bad. Bragging about how you gone take me from my girl and how she must ain't doing something right cuz I ain't at home with her. I'mma teach you about talking shit about shit you don't know nothing about. You ain't taking no dick, ho. And your pussy slaw. ARCH YOUR FUCKING BACK AND TOOT YOUR ASS UP BEFORE I CHOKE YOU THE FUCK OUT FOR WASTING MY DAMN TIME!"

I almost didn't even recognize his voice and him yelling at the woman caught me off guard. I listened as the head board smacked the wall repeatedly and the woman screamed out. Max grunted and then released the long deep moan he does when he nuts. I just shook my head and walked away. I didn't care anything about him standing up for me. Standing up for me didn't require him to stick his dick in that bitch. I didn't even have any sympathy for the fact that she was a lousy fuck. All I knew was that I was tired of mother fuckers getting over on me and taking my kindness for weakness. I was about to teach this nigga a lesson about trying to play me for a fool.

Chapter 15

I decided to fuck Max's head completely up, and I knew exactly how to do it. There was this one guy in particular- a black guy named Eric- who I had been sweet-talking for over two months. He was feeling me on a completely different level. He knew what I was supposed to be all about- sex for hire- but he kept saying he saw something different in me, so much more potential. He wanted to get to know me better. It wasn't so unusual. Some of the guys required a bit of conversation before they actually decided to meet up. But this guy was really into me. It was what it was all the same though. But I was going to use him to prove a point to Max.

I set Eric up as my last date on a Sunday. I had told Max I was cutting this particular Sunday short so I could get some rest, so I only had four dates ahead of him. As I did each date before him, I got more and more excited about what was coming.

When we finished the first four dates, I told Max I was going to go ahead and get ready for the last date, even though we were ahead of schedule and I still had an hour before Eric was supposed to show up. That raised an eyebrow with Max; we usually would go grab something to eat or make small runs if we had spare time between dates. I told him it was nothing. This guy just required a little more finesse. He didn't like it, but he let it go. I hopped in the Audi and went straight to the hotel- not motel- where I planned to meet up with Eric. I had already checked in earlier to keep down suspicion, so I grabbed my bag and went straight up to the room.

I took a shower and lotioned up with the one Bath & Body Works scent that always drove Max crazy: Violet Lily. I sprayed on the matching diamond shimmer body mist. Then I pulled out a La Perla bra and thong set that I knew would have brought Max to his knees. It was black lace, embroidered, and fit perfectly. My breasts were sitting just right and my ass was shiny and plump. I knew Max was going to flip out when he saw me, but that was just a part of the plan.

When Max let himself in with his room key, I had soft music playing from my phone. I had finished my make-up and was still in the bathroom doing my hair when he came in calling my name.

"I'm in here," I shouted to him. He was talking a mile a minute, rambling about some shit that had to do with the drugs but was completely irrelevant at the moment. But when he rounded the corner...

"Shonna, what the fuck?!" I fought back my laughter to keep a straight face.

"What?" I asked nonchalantly as I positioned and pinned curls precisely in the mirror.

"What do you mean 'what'? What the fuck are you doing all this shit for? I understand you're trying to play a role, but you're doing too much for this nigga. It don't require all this shit," he fumed, and I enjoyed it.

"I told you he requires a little more finesse. I gotta make him comfortable or he won't stay long enough for us to do this shit," I explained.

"Hell naw. You're doing the most, though. You got on a thong and shit. What is this? This La Perla? What the fuck, Shonna?"

"Max, you're a guy, so you wouldn't understand. Some guys just require a little more than others. Let me do this. You just handle your end," I blew him off.

"Hell naw, Slim. You're walking around this mother fucker in La Perla for a trick. You really think I'm supposed to be cool with this?"

"I don't care how cool or how heated you are about the shit. Deal with it," I told him as I brushed past him.

"Deal with it?" I heard his feet approaching as he started towards me, but I turned and cut him off.

"You need to get into place and watch your volume because he'll be here any minute." Max stood there looking mad as hell, but defeated.

"This shit ain't over, Shonna. You got me fucked up," he said as he retreated into the bathroom.

"Naw, nigga," I said under my breath. "You got me fucked up. As a matter of fact, I'm about to show you just how fucked up you got me."

I plopped down on the edge of the bed and closed my eyes so I could refocus. Max was in the bathroom talking low on the phone to someone about some kind of product, while I tried to get myself back into the mood that he had killed in the room. I wasn't going to let him mess anything up because I had the entire event completely planned out.

Twenty minutes later, there was knock on the door. Max peeked his head out of the bathroom door, gave the signal with a nod, and then took his position in the bathroom with the door slightly ajar. I smirked as I walked to the door. This was about to be the most fun I had had in months.

Eric came in smelling and looking like a million bucks wrapped in a black Armani suit. I had seen him a couple of times since we had been talking, but he usually was dressed business casual and I would just hop into the passenger seat of his Tahoe so we could talk. Now, here he was towering over my five-foot-four frame standing at six-foot-three with the most beautiful pearly white smile and the most edible creamy milk chocolatey skin I had ever laid eyes upon. Baby, he could get it any time, any day.

He wrapped his arms around me before he even looked me over, but when he stepped back and laid eyes on what I was- or more like wasn't- wearing, the desire shined like stars in his eyes. He handed me a dozen red roses and I damn near soaked my thong. I had never received flowers, let alone roses.

I knew Eric wanted this to be so much more than what it was. He really hadn't been down with paying for sex from the very beginning, but he was feeling me so tough, he settled for it just to be able to have a chance to get close to me. I just couldn't get Eric involved in the shit I had going on. He was a straight by the book law-abiding citizen, and I had become nothing of the sort. Besides, cheater or not, Max was my partner-in-crime.

I turned on the TV as Eric took of his suitcoat and tie. He
sat on the edge of the bed watching me move around the room
while I pretended not to notice.

"C'mere, girl," he said as he gently grabbed my hand
and pulled me to him. I straddled his lap, wrapped my arms
around his neck, and planted a long kiss on him. He held me
close as he kissed me back and then parted my lips with his
tongue and kissed me deeper. His hand slid up the back of my
neck and into my curls as he kissed me and I moaned softly.

I knew Max couldn't hear much from the bathroom with
the TV blaring, but I planned to make sure he heard everything he needed to hear. Max and I had a very strict rule that
he would always remain hidden in the bathroom until I gave
him the code word. Under no circumstances would he ever
come out of the bathroom without the code, and I knew this.
That rule by itself was what I was banking on. It was going to
fuck Max up the most.

"Damn, baby, you smell good as hell," he whispered as
he placed a trail of kisses down my neck and between my
breasts. "And you're looking fucking edible. I've never seen
lingerie like this. What is this?"

"It's La Perla," I whispered.

"La Perla? Ain't that shit expensive?" he frowned.

"Depends on your definition of expensive. It's definitely a
delicacy in the lingerie world."

"You did all of this for me? Or is this the norm? Do you do this for all of your clients?" he asked.

"First of all, you're not just a client," I told him.

"Oh, I'm not?" He raised an eyebrow.

"No," I said as I shook my head. "I'm really feeling you. I did all of this just for you. It's definitely not the norm for me. I can tell you that," I giggled.

"Oh, really? I feel so special," he smiled as he ran his hand up my back.

"You should," I told him.

"I want to make you feel special too," he said. The look in his eye dripped of so much insinuation that he might as well had said he wanted to curl my toes and roll my eyes back.

"How so?" I asked quietly. Eric grabbed my neck just under my chin with a firm grip, tilted my head slightly with his thumb, and kissed down my neck from my earlobe to my shoulder. My breathing grew heavy as I shuddered as I exhaled.

"I wish I could make you mine," he whispered.

"I'm all yours tonight," I said as I looked into his eyes. He stopped and gazed into my eyes and then began unbuttoning his shirt. I kissed up and down his neck until he got his shirt off. He picked me up and laid me on the bed. My heart raced as his fingers unfastened my bra as he placed wet kisses from my chin down to my navel. My mind was on a treadmill. My conscience was repeating over and over that this was really happening and there was no turning back from here.

Eric removed my bra and didn't even hesitate. His eyes closed as his lips wrapped around my right nipple. I heard his shoes tumble to the carpeted floor as I ran my hand over his fresh fade. Part of me was in ecstasy with his lips and tongue caressing my nipple, but the other part of me was praying he had the right size tool for the job I needed handled. He glanced up at me and ran his fingers over my thong, noticing the moisture that had soaked through the silky material.

He stood up and dropped his pants and I didn't even look. I was just going with the flow. He bent down and slid my thong over my hips and my black Jimmy Choos. I knew my lips were glistening in moisture; I didn't even have to look. I knew my pussy was pretty; he didn't even have to say it.

"Oh my God," he whispered, and then immediately put his face in it. My eyes instantly rolled back and my back arched involuntarily. It had been a while since Max had eaten the cookies, but Eric was making up for every second of lost time. It was obvious that he enjoyed what he was doing. I watched as his neck rolled and his tongue swirled, and thought I was going to pull up the whole sheet when his tongue flicked back and forth quickly. Eric looked up into my eyes just as the pleasure became too much and I tried to back away from him a bit.

"Unh-unh," he shook his head. "Don't run from me, baby. Don't fight it. I want you to bust as many nuts as you can. Bring that pretty ass pussy here, baby," he said as he wove his arms through my legs and tightened his grip so I couldn't move away from him. He held me tight until my back arched, my legs shook, and I screamed out in pleasure.

He came up with his lips shining and curled into a smile. I opened the nightstand and pulled out two condoms and handed him one. He ripped it open with his teeth as he slid his boxers off and then slid the condom on smoothly. I took a deep breath to prepare myself, closed my eyes to keep the surrealness of the moment, and then held my breath to prevent myself from crying out in unbearable pleasure as he slid himself inside of me.

It was perfect. It was everything and so much more. He was just the right width to make me feel him against all of my walls, just the right length to be pleasurably uncomfortable. Starting off slow, he stroked it deep, his head pushing deep into a spot that had never been touched before. Seeing how good it felt to me and how well I was taking the dick, he put my legs up over his shoulders and bounced even deeper inside of me.

"Oh, Eric, shit!" I screamed out. There was no faking anything with him. I didn't have to put on a front for effect. I was in heaven and I knew Max could hear it in my voice.

"Does it feel good, baby?" he asked as he leaned down, pushing my knees against my cheeks, and kissed my lips.

"Yes, baby. Yes, yes. Oh, God!"

"You want it deeper?" he asked.

"Ooohhh, yes, baby!" I moaned.

"Turn over for me," he whispered as he let my legs down and slid himself out of me.

I turned over, backed my ass up against his dick to show him I wanted it just as much as he did, and then arched my back with my ass up high and my shoulders down low.

"Grab that pillow to make yourself more comfortable," he instructed me as he kissed up and down my back while running his fingertips over my sides and my breasts. "I'm going to warn you ahead of time. I'm about to stroke you so good, so deep, so perfect that you're going to cum harder than you've probably ever nutted in your whole life. Then I'm going to fuck the shit out of you until you nut on this dick again."

"Eric-"

"No," he said as he gripped my hips. "Ain't no running, no fighting it, no negotiation. I aim to please, and believe me, I can tell exactly what you need. I've already figured out exactly where your spot is. Toot that ass up and grip that pillow. I got you, baby. You haven't been fucked right in a long time and I can tell. But I got you tonight, baby. I'm gone get you right."

He slid back inside of my womb and I inhaled sharply. Each stroke was slow torture. Every single moan I released was impassioned. He hit my spot over and over again with a slow, steady rhythm. He was confident, strong, and forceful. Every stroke was packed with power and pushed out of me a cry of pleasure that I rarely was able to reproduce.

"How does it feel, baby?" he asked.

"Don't stop, baby."

"Shit is good, ain't it?"

"Oh, God, Eric. Don't stop," I was just barely able to squeeze out.

"Nut on this dick, baby. Nut hard on this dick. I want you to get that nut you haven't been getting," he told me. He swirled his hips in a circle and hit an entirely different spot and I felt like I was losing my damn mind.

"Eric!" I screamed out. This nigga had me calling his name.

"That's it, baby. Get that nut. That's what this dick is for: to give you that satisfaction you really need."

"Oh, Eric. Oh, Eric," I grunted. I never grunted. I always moaned, always screamed, but I never grunted. He was giving me a pleasure from so deep down inside that I was damn-near cross-eyed and drooling.

"That's it, baby. Get it. Get it," he said quietly.

"Oh! Oh! Eric! Eric! Eriiiiiiiccc!" And I heard the juices as they secreted out of me. He gripped my hips tighter and exhaled.

"Get ready, baby, because I'm about to give it to you. Don't fight the nut because I'm going to get it out of you whether you want it to come or not. Toot it up, grip the pillow, and bust this nut," he said.

And with that, he commenced to fucking the shit out of me with strong, deep, hard thrusts. I was screaming out, "Yes! Yes! Yes!"

"Take this dick, girl," he demanded.

"Give it to me, baby!"

"Take it. Take it. Take it!" he grunted.

"Fuck me! Fuck me! Oh, shit!"

"That's it! Bust this nut! I feel it. I feel you. Don't fight it!"

"Oh, Eric, fuck!"

"Shit! I'm about to pop off too, baby. Nut on this dick again for me." He hit it even harder, even faster, and I gave up. There was no fighting it or any type of holding back at that point. I released a scream I had never heard come from my body before and so much juice poured from my womb that it formed a puddle on the sheet. The tight grip of my walls in the midst of my orgasm forced Eric over the edge as well. He growled loudly and I felt the surge of heat deep within as his own juices released into the condom.

We collapsed onto the bed, and I laid there, my breathing

heavy, my eyes closed, my mind racing. I knew Max must have been fuming. He probably was seeing red and had steam pouring from his ears. There is no man on this earth who can truly maintain his sanity while the visual of his woman being fucked in the doggie-style position is etched in his head. Men already can't stand the thought of another man dipping into his cookie jar, but the thought of his woman bent over with her ass up and another man drilling her from behind will drive a man over the very edge of the cliff of insanity. I knew that Max was probably clutching his glock so tight his knuckles were white. That thought tickled my soul.

I glanced over at Eric and discovered he was watching me. Not in a creepy way. He was just lying there studying my facial features, following the curves of my frame, memorizing my flesh. The look in his eye told of the adoration he had for me, the desire that was still there even though he had just had me.

"You want a towel to clean up?" I whispered to him.

"No, I'm good," he said as he wrapped the used condom up in paper towels and dropped it in the waste basket next to the bed. "I'm going to hop in the shower when I get home." He leaned over and kissed down my collarbone. "Damn, you taste so sweet."

"Thank you," I whispered, genuinely flattered.

"Am I going to be able to see you again? Are you going to let me steal you away for a little while?"

"Most definitely," I said as I nodded.

He rose to his feet and began getting redressed, and for the first time, I wished that he was mine and Max wasn't hiding in the bathroom so that maybe Eric could stay a little longer.

"Most definitely, huh?" he smirked. "Alright, alright," he nodded, obviously happily relieved. "Well," he said as he reached into his pants pocket for his billfold. I had been getting dressed as well and was pulling a t-shirt over my head. "How much do I owe you?" he asked as he pulled a small fan of one hundred dollar bills from his billfold. I walked up to him and put my right hand gently on top of his left.

"Keep your money, baby. You don't owe me anything," I said quietly.

"Are you… are you sure?" he frowned.

"I'm positive," I nodded. "You don't owe me a thing."

"Well, oh… okay," he hesitated. "Well, I'll see you soon then?"

"C'mon, I'll walk you downstairs," I told him as I grabbed my bag. "You'll definitely be seeing me again very soon," I told him as we walked to the elevator.

"Good. Great," he beamed as he pressed the button for the elevator. "Slim, you are amazing. You're perfect in every way. You're intelligent, and your sex game is on point. You're slim in the waist and thick in all the right places. Slim thick, witcho cute ass," he chuckled.

"'Slim thick.' That's cute," I giggled as the elevator door

opened. I pushed him into the elevator and kissed him passionately as the doors closed. "Thank you so much, baby. Thank you, thank you, thank you."

"No, baby. Thank you. And whenever you want it, whenever you need me, I'm here, at your service."

"I'm going to hold you to that," I assured him. The elevator dinged, the door opened, and we stepped out. "I'll see you soon," I told him. He grabbed my hand gently.

"I hope so," he said as he released it and we went our separate ways.

I left Max's ass up there in that hotel room and went home. My phone began ringing a half an hour later. Max. It rang every fifteen minutes after that until I turned my phone off two hours later. I wanted him to be mad. I wanted him to be pissed. I wanted him to hurt like I hurt when I heard him fucking that woman in that hotel room like I wasn't at home wishing he would spend time with me. I wanted him to be just as offended as I was that he would give me something he had promised was only mine to someone else. And more than anything, I wanted him to realize that I was a fucking savage and he had me fucked up. I wanted him to realize that I was not the one to be toyed with, that I played the same game and I came to win. I wanted him to realize that I had the same capabilities that he had- that I could betray him, break him down, and destroy him just as easily as he thought he could hide a betrayal that he knew could possibly destroy me.

I laid in my California king sized bed that night and felt more satisfied with my own decisions and actions than I had during our whole relationship. From that day on, I was no longer Shonna. I was Slim Thick. I was that bitch. I never gave anyone else my real name. All they knew was Slim Thick and if they ever went to the police- and some of their dumb asses did- the only name they had to offer them was Slim Thick.

Chapter 16

I was awakened at eight the next morning by the resounding banging on my kitchen door. I took my time throwing a silk robe over my nakedness as I walked to the door. I opened the wood door just as Max was about to beat on the glass again. I turned lock on the storm door, twisted the knob, and turned and walked off while rubbing my eyes. I was almost immediately stopped in my tracks and snatched backwards by my hair as Max threw me into a headlock. He caught me off guard and I returned the favor.

Max had his arm wrapped tight around my neck, attempting with all his might to choke the life out of me. Time slowed down to a creep and my mind cleared itself of all thoughts. My hand slipped into my robe and ripped my .45 from my thigh holster. I reached between my legs and shoved the barrel against the crotch of Max's pants.

"Max," I choked, "I'm only going to say this one time. I can't breathe. If you don't let me go, I promise you, if you choke me out, the last thing I'm going to do with my last breath before I lose consciousness is blow your whole damn dick off."

Max's body stiffened and his grip tightened slightly and then slowly released me. I stood up firmly on my feet while clutching my throat, trying to rub away the pain. A fierce rage shot through my body to my core and I spun around and smacked Max so hard with the .45 that the entire right side of his face immediately swelled. He doubled over and screamed out in agonizing pain. I took that opportunity to knee him in the face and then kick him in the crotch.

"Problem number one: don't you EVER put your fucking hands on me, bitch!" I said as I approached him again. "Problem number two: you reap what the fuck you sew, ho!" I kicked him in the gut. "Problem number three: it's too goddamned early in the fucking morning for this bullshit!"

I sat the gun on the kitchen island and leaned on the island with one hand on the gun and the other on my hip.

"You have real deal lost your fucking mind," I told him, "barging up in my house and attacking me like I couldn't have predicted that shit. I bet you didn't predict my little cute ass being strapped, though, did you? Bitch, I'm always on point," I taunted him. "And to think I was willing to talk to you about this shit, but I don't even want to rap now. Not after this shit. You can roll, bruh, and when you're ready to talk like adults, call me." I stood there waiting for him to pick himself up off the floor, but he stayed there on his knees breathing hard and dropping tears.

"Bitch, you got me fucked up," he huffed.

"So you gone keep talking shit? You gone sit here on my kitchen floor holding your nuts talking shit? Do I need to shut your ass up? Let me know now because I have a bomb ass judo chop that will silence you for the rest of the day," I threatened.

"Shonna-"

"Just roll, bruh. Just roll. I don't want to talk right now."

I watched him pick himself up off the floor and limp out the door. A mixture of emotions washed over me. I burst into laughter at just how pitiful he looked and how off-guard I had caught him, but that quickly gave way to the hurt and the anger that Max had actually put his hands on me and that he had cheated on me. I was over the entire scene. I climbed back into the bed, rolled my eyes at Curtis' smiling face on the bedroom wall, and then went back to sleep.

* ～ * ～ *

I didn't hear from Max again until Thursday. I was driving home after taking a trip to Miami to retrieve the contents of yet another safe deposit box when my phone rang and Max's name and picture popped up on my screen. I took a deep breath and picked up the phone.

"Hello?"

"Shonna."

"Yeah, what's up?"

"Ummm, I came over so we could talk, but you aren't here."

"Yeah, I had a little bit of running to do," I lied, but I'm on my way to the house now."

"You don't have to come back now just because I'm here. Go ahead and finish handling your business, and we can link up later."

"I'm actually done and I'm already on my way home. I've been out and about since about eight-thirty," I said as I looked at the clock and observed that it was ten minutes until noon. "If you can hold on about five to ten minutes, I'll be pulling up."

"Alright, I'm here in the driveway," he said.

I pulled over two blocks down the street from the house and crammed all of the bags I had thrown across the back seat into the trunk. I took my black duffle bag and black Victoria's Secret tote and shoved them all the way to the back of the trunk first and then loaded everything else on top of them, got back into the car, and drove up the winding driveway and into the garage. I didn't look at or speak to Max as I grabbed my purse, unlocked the door, and went into the house. I sat down at the island and crossed my legs in my Valentino sundress and waited as he came in and closed and locked the door. He came around the island and sat down as well, leaving a stool between us to keep a comfortable distance.

"Hey," he said nervously.

"What's up?" I answered nonchalantly.

"I… ummm… I don't know where to start," he said quietly. "I think the first thing that should come out of my mouth should be an apology. That should be first and foremost. So, Shonna, I want to tell you I'm sorry for everything I've done wrong and every bit of hurt I've caused you in any way."

"I accept you apology, Max," I said.

"I also want to apologize for under-estimating you in every way that I have. Your capabilities outstretch my imagination by miles, and I doubted that and took it for granted, and I'm sorry."

"I accept that apology as well."

"I've done quite a bit of thinking over the past few days and the one thing I just can't get past is how much I truly and sincerely miss you," he said as he looked me in my eyes. "We haven't even really been apart for an abnormal amount of time, but the disconnect that exists between us has made the few days we've been out of sync feel like an eternity. You and I have always been excellent about having open lines of communication, but the last few days have really been the opposite. It wasn't that I couldn't call you, but I just felt like I shouldn't. I've never felt like that with you, and I never want to. It's a terrible, heart-breaking feeling," he explained, "and I almost fell into a panic because of it."

I looked up at Max and noticed how intensely he was studying me as he spoke. His eyes were narrowed, but sad. His lips were moving, but still formed a frown.

"Max, all of this is very poetic and sounds great. You've always been eloquent and had a way with words, but you and I both know you ain't saying shit right now," I told him. I turned to face him completely. "Why don't you say what you really want to say, how you really feel? Why don't you go ahead and curse and yell and scream? I've got some good china in the cabinets. I don't think I'd die if you broke a few plates." Max looked at me like I had lost my mind. "See, all of this sounds good," I whispered, "but it's bullshit, and it's not going to get either of us or this relationship anywhere. Go ahead and say what you really want to say so that you don't end up throwing it in my face in an argument a month from now. Go ahead and get the shit off your chest, Max, because I don't need no surprises."

"Surprises? You want to talk about surprises? How about the surprise I got when I was sitting here waiting for an Audi to pull up the driveway and you pulled up in some nigga's Porsche?!" he spat at me. I cringed. I had been so frantic to hide the bags and luggage from my trip that I had forgotten all about the fact that I had retrieved the Porsche Cayenne from a storage unit at a self-storage facility after I found the keys and information in the safe deposit box in Miami. I hadn't even thought about the fact that I was in a car Max had never seen before.

"That car belongs to me," I told him.

"Yeah right, Shonna," he scowled. "We've been together all this time and I've never seen that damn car before, in the driveway, in the garage, on the street, nothing. So the mother fucker just appeared out of thin air?"

"No, I bought it yesterday on a pretty good deal," I lied.

"You bought it? It belongs to you?" he said in evident disbelief. "Quit fucking lying."

"What reason do I have to lie, Max? I'm telling you the truth. The Porsche, along with the Audi and the Range, all belong to me. And I'd appreciate it if you'd stop trying to divert the conversation and get down to the real topic at hand because this calm bullshit you're doing right now is fake as fuck and it's starting to piss me off. So cut the crap and come on with the real problem so we can get this over with."

"But, baby-"

"No, no, no!" I stopped him. "Don't you 'but baby' me. A few days ago I was the bitch you were trying to choke out right here in this same kitchen. Now, you fucking miss me?" I scoffed. "See, Max, all this beating around the bush ain't gone get us nowhere except the bottom of a pile of unresolved problems. Honestly, do I look like I have the time or patience to deal with a bunch of bullshit and fakery?"

"Shonna, I didn't come here for that. We can discuss our problems later. I came here to apologize and make amends."

"Later? Why put off for tomorrow what you can do today? Is this shit that hard for you? How hard can it really be to just be honest? What do you want? You want me to start it off? Huh? Do I need to set the tone? Because I refuse to ride this merry-go-round of avoidance and pretend with you. It's just now what I do," I told him.

"Well, let's hear how I really feel then, Shonna, since you already know. Doesn't look like I need to say much. It seems you've got it all figured out already."

"So this is the game you want to play? What do I need to do? Say something to strike a nerve? Cut you deep to get you to snap back to reality? Why don't you say something real, Max? Like how you're sorry for putting me in a headlock, but you really did want to choke me out. Like how you love me and you feel more betrayed than you've ever felt in your life. Why don't we start with how bad you wish I was a nigga so you could get a one-on-one with me after that shit I pulled at the hotel? Where do you want to start, Max? Pick a place!" I shouted.

"You're goddamned right I wish I could beat your fucking ass behind that shit," he growled. "Do you know how demeaning it is to stand there and listen to the person you love fucking someone else? Do you know how low I felt? I felt like I wasn't shit, like I wasn't enough, like I wasn't good enough. You didn't give a fuck about the fact that I was standing on the other side of that door and you were killing me. You don't know what that felt like!"

"Who doesn't know? Who? Me?" I burst into a fit of maniacal laughter and Max frowned in confusion. "Night after night of me asking you to spend time with me. So many times I've looked at you and told you I want you to fuck me. How many times did I tell you I wanted you to fuck the shit out of me with no remorse?"

"But that's no excuse for you to do what you did!"

"It may not be! But to stand on the other side of that door and hear flesh slapping flesh, moans, grunts, screams-"

"Something you know nothing about-"

"Of another woman while the man who swears he loves me fucks her like there's no fucking tomorrow... fucks her like I'm not at home wishing he was there with me, wishing he would fuck me the way he was fucking her..." Max's jaw dropped and he was speechless.

"Shonna…"

"Don't you call my name now! You weren't thinking about me when you were sticking dick to that ugly ass, nothing ass ho, now were you? I don't know how it feels? You don't know how it feels to truly trust someone- just one someone- and they really betray you like that. And that bitch wasn't even worth it! She wasn't even half of me! She can't even take dick!" I yelled.

"Oh my God, Shonna," Max whispered. "Baby, I'm so sorry. I'm so sorry. I didn't know…"

"That's right. You didn't know and you were going to sit here and play the victim like I had just done you so wrong for no damn reason. I bet you were going to lay it on thick about how hurt and traumatized you were. The truth is that you deserved that shit. I did to you the same shit you did to me," I said with a tear escaping from each eye. "You want to talk about hurt and pain now?" I chuckled. "Ha! Well, at least I got you to tell the truth."

"Shonna, baby, I'm so sorry…"

"You can keep your apology. You're not sorry. You're only sorry you got caught." I shook my head. "I hope that shit benefitted you because it cost you more than you can imagine," I told him. "One thing holds true though. What's good for the goose is good for the gander."

"Say what?"

"If you don't give a fuck, neither do I. If you're going to fuck off, I am too. All of this 'do as I say, not as I do' ass shit is for the birds. I'm just as grown as you. Two can play this mother fucking game."

"This shit is not a game, Shonna. You think you're supposed to just be able to fuck whoever you want to fuck and I'm supposed to be okay with it?"

"Why not? Huh? That's what you think. You think you're supposed to be able to stick your dick in whatever bitch will turn the corner of her skirt up for you, and I'm supposed to be oblivious to it and if I do know, I'm supposed to turn the other cheek. Is that how you want to live? Is that how you want this to go? Because if that's the game you want to play, I'm going to play that mother fucker too. You just be ready," I pointed my finger at him, "because I play to win."

"You're supposed to be mine."

"And you're supposed to be mine, but you threw all of that shit out the window."

"Shonna, baby, I'm sorry."

"Sorry? Nigga, you ain't sorry. You can miss me with your fake ass apology. You're not sorry. What the fuck do you have to be sorry about? The only thing you did was stumble upon a woman who had just lost the only man she had ever loved in the worst way possible. Then you befriended her, made her trust you when she trusted absolutely no one else in the whole world, convinced her to become involved in a committed relationship with you at a point in her life where she should have been finding herself, focusing on herself, and healing, and then caused her even more pain by betraying her trust. That's all you did. Nothing to be sorry about," I said sarcastically.

"I said I'm sorry, Shonna. What do you want me to do? I can't go back in time and change it. I'm trying to apologize to you!"

"You think I want an apology? You think an apology is going to fix this? Fuck your apology!" I screamed.

"Shonna, you ain't no fucking saint either. You could've caught me and called me out on my bullshit. Hell, that would've been enough punishment- just the embarrassment of knowing that you knew. But no! What did you do? You jumped to the extreme and did a revenge fuck with me listening from the bathroom just to get back at me! You could've come out on top, but instead, you ain't no better than me," Max said as he paced the kitchen floor.

"Me being a bigger person was never an option. I'm too mother fucking petty for that shit. And I did come out on top. My entire goal was to inflict the same pain on you that you inflicted on me. I accomplished just that. I didn't give a fuck about your feelings just like you didn't give a fuck about mine. I wanted you to feel just as low, as worthless, as disgusted, as degraded as I felt standing on the other side of that hotel room door, and I did that shit. That's what the fuck you get!" I was heartless, completely emotionless, and utterly unmoved by Max's pain. Sugar-coating shit for him was not going to help our situation, so I told him the ugly ass truth.

"Shonna, you're fucked up. You know that? You're a real

fuck up ass person," he told me with squinted watery eyes. I stood there amused, wondering if I was supposed to be offended.

"Thank you," I said with pride. He scoffed at me in shock. "So now," I said simply, "what are we going to do about the situation?"

"What do you mean?"

"You done with me?" I looked into his eyes.

"Honestly, I should probably be asking you that. I started this big ass mess. I sparked the fire that turned into this inferno," he said as he shook his head. "Baby, for what it's worth, I really am sorry."

"I accept your apology, Maximillian," I said resolutely.

"Thank you, Shoshonna," he was barely able to whisper. "Will you… can I have another chance… please?"

"Max, if I go back down this road with you, I want you to understand you don't get a third chance."

"I understand."

"I've never been so betrayed and so disrespected in my entire life," I heard my voice crack. "I never had to worry about this with Curtis." I felt tears begin to roll down my cheeks, and it angered me. "You come along just months after I lost my best friend, my husband, my everything, and you think it's just okay for you to do me like this. You're damned right I got you back. I'd have been a fool not to." I took a deep breath and looked Max straight in the eyes and said, "You pull anything like this shit again and you'll regret it for the rest of your life."

Chapter 17

"Bitch, where the fuck you been?"

It was too damn early in the morning for this shit. Why didn't I just let it ring…again?

"Dee, don't start-"

"Bitch, don't 'Dee, don't start this shit' me. Where the fuck you been, why haven't you been answering my calls, and why haven't you called me back?"

I knew I had fucked up. I had fucked up months ago that first time I had hit ignore on her call. Instead of fixing the situation, I just kept hitting ignore every time she called, and now, it had been at least seven or eight months since we had spoken.

Over the course of my activities with Max, I had been called a lot of different pet names. "Mi amor," "Sugar," "Baby Girl," "Honey," "Lil Momma." But no matter who tried and how many times, I never let anyone call me Sunshine. Sunshine was off limits because Sunshine came in the form of my best friend, Dakota.

Dakota and I had been best friends since middle school, and we knew each other like our times tables. She was five-foot-three, a hundred and thirty-five pounds, thick in the waist, and cute in the face. She had the beauty of Super Girl and the personality of Harley Quinn. She was innocent as hell, but at even the suggestion or mention of crazy, she turned into the most criminally maniacal bitch you could ever imagine.

I hadn't told Dakota what I had been doing with Max because I knew she would kill me. I had always been the most innocent, safe-playing, by-the-book, law-abiding citizen possible, and here I was dope-dealing and robbing Mexicans. Dakota wouldn't kill me if she found out; she'd flat out murder me.

The problem was that I needed Dakota. Of course, she was my best friend and I always told her everything, so I needed her for that, but I also need to bring her into my operation. I had been talking to a few guys who had offered to pay me incredible amounts of money for threesomes. Of course, they'd never get them, but the promise of the fantasy being fulfilled was returned by the promise that these guys would have larger knots in their pockets when they showed up.

"Dakota, can you not today?" I said groggily as I rolled over.

"What do you mean can I not today? What's so special about today other than the fact that you decided to answer the phone for me after I haven't spoken to you in a year," she fussed.

"It has not been a damn year, Dakota. Stop exaggerating," I said as I rolled my eyes in the darkness.

"Damn near! Shit, you already done moved and ain't tell me where the fuck you stay. I can't even come by to see you, let alone check to make sure your ass is still alive. Then you're not picking up when I call or returning any of my messages. I'm going to strangle your mother fucking ass when I see you. Maybe if I cut off your air supply it'll have the opposite effect on you and reverse your fucked up ass brain cells."

She was always so extreme. She never threatened me like a normal person. She always had to paint a picture of just how near death she was going to bring me before she showed mercy upon me and so graciously allowed me to live. I shook my head.

"Bitch, you ain't gone do shit. Cut the bullshit out. What's up though?"

"Shit. What's been up with you? What have you been up to?"

"Nothing much," I lied.

"That ain't what I heard. I heard you haven't been back to Nike since Curtis died," she said.

"Well, you heard right then."

"So what are you doing for money? How are you paying your bills?"

"I've got some other stuff going on that I've been getting by with."

"What the fuck does that mean, Shonna? Why are you talking in code?"

"Look, write down my address. You got a pen and paper?"

"Yeah. Go ahead with it," she huffed. I gave her my address and told her to come by my house after she got off work.

When I hung up from her, I looked at my phone and realized that it was two in the afternoon and I had slept all day. I rolled out of the bed and hopped in the shower before heading to the kitchen to start on dinner for the two of us.

*　～　*　～　*

It took one hell of a dinner and a whole lot of convincing and persuading, but I finally got Dakota to agree to assist me in my activities. Ironically, she had demanded to meet Max before she consented to anything, and he happened to pop up at the house while she was there. He sat and broke down the dynamics of the operation to her and she eventually gave in.

Max eventually left to allow us to enjoy our girl time, but as soon as he did, Dakota lit into me. She kept demanding to know how I had gotten the house and how I was able to keep it up with no job. I refused to taint anyone's image of Curtis, including Dakota's as she had known him well, so I insisted that it was a rental and that I had discovered that Curtis had a small life insurance policy. Of course, she didn't buy it, but she had no choice but to accept my answer because it was the only one I was offering.

Dakota jumped in head first and was almost immediately completely submerged in the game. She was still working her regular job during the week, just like Max and I were still trying to get rid of the last of the product we had. On the weekends, we would usually have one or two plays for threesomes, and Dakota was always down for those. Dakota was single and kinky, and she always enjoyed torturing the guys a little bit sexually before we jacked them. She even got into the habit of going a step further and kissing the guys, but I told her she had to stop that shit because everybody's mouth isn't clean.

One particular night, the three of us were pulling the same move we had pulled dozens of time on a Mexican who claimed he had a dick bigger than most black guys. Maybe he hadn't watched enough porn, but I highly doubted he was accurate with his description. Dakota and I got him up in the room at this little motel that wanted to be a real hotel so bad that they even had a fat, lazy security guard who was supposed to be patrolling the parking lot, but spent most of his shift asleep in his company-assigned Chevrolet S-10. We were playing the part. Dakota got him out of his pants while I got him out of his shirt while feeling up his chest. He was loving the little situation he was in.

"You're such a fucking hunk," I told him, and he chuckled just like most guys did when I said that. If they only knew that was the code word for what would happen next, they wouldn't have found it so cute.

Max busted out of the bathroom with his .45 cocked and ready, and Dakota and I both snatched matching chrome .9mm's from the foot of the bed.

"Put your mother fucking hands up, don't move, and nobody gets hurt," Max instructed calmly, almost cordially, as he began the same speech he had given a hundred times. "Slim Thick is going to stand just like this with her gun pointed at the tip of your nose and I'm going to reach into the pocket of your pants there and remove your cash. While we're both busy with that-her with keeping a steady aim and me with filling my fists- Sunshine over here is going to go start up the car. You be calm, don't move, don't try to pull anything, and no one gets hurt. You'll lose a little money, but, hey! What's a little money compared to your life? Huh? Sooo… Sunshine, if you don't mind," he said as Dakota caught the car keys he tossed to her and walked out the door. "Great! Now Slim Thick, if you would keep that barrel pointed straight and steady," he said as he approached our scared little Mexican friend.

He bent down next to the bed and stuck his hand into the back pocket of the pair of jeans that had just been tossed to the floor minutes before. There was a sudden fast shift on the bed as the guy pulled a gun from behind a pillow. Max looked up from the very large wad of money he was pulling from the pants pocket with a look of shocking satisfaction only to receive a spray of cherry red blood across his face.

"Slim!" he gasped as I lowered the gun. His first concern was me, obviously, because he jumped up from next to the bed and leaped across the bed to make sure I was okay. I wasn't even shaken. I stood there just as calm and cool as I had been before I pulled the trigger while Max felt me up, examining me for bullet holes that were non-existent. "Slim, are you okay?" he huffed.

"Yep," I said nonchalantly, "I'm fine. You okay?" I asked as I looked him over. I should've been considerably more concerned about his well-being than he was about mine, given the pistol that has just been en route to being pointed at his head.

"I'm…ummm…I'm cool," he said. "C'mon! We gotta go. Somebody is going to call and the police will be pulling up in a second."

For all of ten seconds, I was stuck in space. My eyes were glued to the gaping hole I had just blown into this man's face. His nose was gone, along with most of the right side of his face. There was blood spatter and brain matter all over the headboard behind him, and blood drenched the sheets. My mind immediately flashed back to the moment Curtis was killed, and my heart skipped a beat.

"Slim, let's go! We gotta go!" Max's voice jerked me back into reality and my mind greeted the rude awakening that was the here and now.

I snatched up all of our belongings, which we always kept to a minimum, and my feet barely touched the ground as I followed Max out the door. Dakota was waiting at the bottom of the steps with the car running. Max and I hopped into the car and Dakota snatched off the parking lot and flew down the street.

"I heard a gunshot. Was that y'all?" Dakota frowned at me sitting next to her as she drove.

"Shonna shot the nigga," Max said from the back seat.

"Shonna! You didn't!" Dakota looked back and forth between me and the road as she got onto the interstate.

"I didn't have a choice! The nigga pulled a gun from behind the pillow. He was going to kill Max. I did what I had to do," I said and then shrugged my shoulders.

"Oh, shit, Shonna!" Dakota whined. "Did you kill him? Is he dead?" she asked. I was silent as I watched her eyes dart back and forth between me, the road, and Max's reflection in the rearview mirror. I could tell she read the lyrics to the song in Max's eyes and her entire facial expression changed. "Oh, God, Shonna! You didn't. Tell me you didn't kill him! Oh, God! We're going to jail. Shit, we're going to jail!"

"Calm down, Dee. We're not going to jail. Nobody saw us, and the police won't be able to connect us to this shit," I assured her.

"But, Shonna, you just killed somebody! People don't get away with murder, Shonna. And this wasn't even planned. We weren't even careful and I know we all left prints in that room."

"Oh, please, Dee! How many other prints are in that filthy ass room? They'll be pulling up prints from people who stayed in that room three months ago. Stop being such a worry wart and drive this damn car," I told her.

"How can you be so fucking calm?" she shouted.

"Why are you so theatrical? You didn't shoot the mother fucker. I did. I wouldn't let you take the fall for me anyway, and you know this. Max is my man. I did what I had to do to protect him. I would've done the same for you. We're a team. We're in this together. I wasn't going to just stand there while he took my nigga's head off. Fuck that shit and fuck that nigga too!"

"Max, you're awfully quiet back there," Dakota said as she looked at him in the rearview mirror. "What do you have to say about all of this?"

"Honestly, I'm too busy counting this knot to be concerned about a dead nigga in a hotel room. Shonna knows I appreciate what she did, and she knows I'd do the same for her in a heartbeat. All of this is understood without the discussion," he said in a monotonous tone that caught my attention as well.

"You sound very preoccupied," I said as I turned around in the passenger seat. I gasped at the stack on Max's lap. "How much money is that?"

"Well, I've counted eighteen thousand so far. It looks like it's going to be a total of twenty thousand dollars, all hundred dollar bills," he revealed.

"Oh my mother fucking God!" I whispered.

"What the fuck…" Dakota mumbled. "Why did he have that much money on him?"

"I don't know," Max chuckled, "but I'm certainly glad he did. Rest in peace to the lil 'migo with the big wad."

"Dakota, don't miss the exit," I told her as I directed her off of the interstate.

"I'm not getting off here. I'm taking the long way in case someone is following us."

"Bitch, why would someone be following us?" I shook my head.

"Have you seen anyone following us?" Max inquired.

"No, but you can never be too careful. Carelessness with your own life will lead to your demise."

"That was a good one." I grinned. "Who said that?"

"I did," she said as she smiled and took the next exit off the interstate.

Chapter 18

The next few days brought heavy news coverage of the young Hispanic male who was discovered shot to death in a hotel room in northeastern Memphis by housekeeping the next morning. Records showed that officers had responded to several reports of shots fired from the area, but had been unable to locate anything unusual because none of the callers could provide a room number and none of them left their names or wanted to speak with police. The real issue arose one morning when Max came knocking on my door at eight in the morning.

"Max, it's the crack of dawn. Why are you here so early?" I asked as I opened the door still rubbing my eyes.

"Slim, you have to get ready to get out of here," he said with his hands deep in his pockets.

"What are you talking about, Max? Get out of here and go where?" I giggled lightly.

"Anywhere, but you can't stay here," he said with urgency in his tone.

"This is my house. What do you mean I can't stay here? What's going on?" I frowned at him with my arms folded across my chest.

"That guy you killed… he was an off-duty undercover police officer. The TBI is taking over the investigation. It's been all over the news since they released the information.

You know the press loves police scandals. They eat that shit up," he told me. I stood there leaning against the kitchen island in shock. An undercover officer? Max and Dakota were both right, I told myself. I couldn't stay here, and I was going to jail.

"Oh, shit," I whispered.

"Go turn on the TV, Shonna. It's been breaking news all morning."

I went into my bedroom and turned on the TV. It was breaking news on every news channel. The TBI was doing a press conference about the case, stating that the victim's identification had been taken with his wallet in what appeared to be a robbery attempt and the coroner had identified him by using his fingerprints. I sat on the edge of the bed deep in thought.

"How long do you think I have?" I looked into Max's eyes as he stood next to me.

"I'm not sure, but you know that with the TBI in-volved, the shit is going to move fast. You need to be making preparations."

"Ok, well, I'll hop on it," I told him resolutely. "I'm going to lay back down for a while. Are you staying?"

"'Lay back down'? Shonna, do you hear yourself? Have you lost your fucking mind? You need to be packing shit and making calls," he shouted at me.

"Max, I'm tired, and this shit is urgent, but it's not an emergency. Unless I need to be out of here within the next few hours, I have time to lay back down for a second. Now are you staying or are you leaving?"

"I'm glad you're making light of this shit, but I'm not. I'm gone. I've got to pack clothes and shit," he said as he pulled his keys from his pocket and headed towards the door.

"What are you packing up for?" I frowned at his back.

"What do you mean? Do you think I'm going to let you run by yourself? I need to be ready whenever we have to jet."

"So you're going with me?"

"There's no way I'd let you run by yourself. We're in this shit together," he turned and said to me.

"Okay, well, when I get up, I'll start making preparations," I assured him.

"Hop on it, Shonna," he said in almost a whisper. "We don't know how long we have, and you don't want to be caught off guard."

"I gotcha. Soon as I get up. I promise," I said. We kissed, Max left, and I went back to bed. "Just because you don't have an emergency exit plan doesn't mean I don't," I said as I climbed back underneath the sheet and comforter and dozed off.

* ~ * ~ *

When I woke up that afternoon, I immediately started making moves. Dakota had already texted me several times about the update on the case, so I called her first.

"Dakota, look, I gotta make this quick because I have a lot to do. I'm going to bring all of my cars over to your house in about an hour. A tractor trailer is going to pull up and load the cars up and ship them somewhere for me. The only thing I need you to do is drive my cars into the containers. Leave the keys in the ignition of each one and lock the doors. You got me?" I gave her quick instructions.

"Yeah, cool. But how are you going to get back home?" she asked.

"Don't worry about it. I got it," I told her.

When I hung up from her, I called Big Bang and Goose on a conference call.

"Bang, I've got some big jars of Percocets, Lortabs, and morphine pills I need to get rid of. I've sold everything else and you two already put in for the last of the weed I have," I told them.

"So what do you need us to do, Slim?" Goose asked. I could hear one of them counting money in the background as I talked. I had already counted twenty-two hundred with him.

"I've got a lot of business I have to handle out of town. If I leave y'all the pills to sell, can I trust y'all to make my drop?"

"Of course, Slim. You know we got you," Big Bang said just a little too eagerly.

"No, you tried it. It didn't work. Don't make me remind you what happened when you tried to get me the first time," I told Big Bang.

"Naw, Slim. We're good," Goose cut in. "We'll handle the business for you. No bullshit."

"Okay," I sighed. "Look, I'm trusting the two of y'all with this shit because you both know how I do business. I know neither one of you will try to play with my money. Am I right?"

"Ain't no games. We got you," Goose said.

"Bang?"

"You got my word, Slim," he assured me.

"Alright because I assure you, I don't care how far away I am, I can touch you. Even if I have to reach out and touch you myself. And believe me, if I have to come see you myself, you'll wish I had just sent somebody. Don't make me send somebody. Please don't make me do it," I told them.

"We got you, Slim," Goose chuckled. "You're in good hands."

"Alright. I'm about to be on my way to y'all," I told them.

When I got off the phone with them, I made a string of calls while packing and loading every single pill and every single bud into the Range Rover for my final drug transaction. I had learned long ago to handle my own business and move in silence. Though Max's help was convenient, I never needed him. Everything that I did, I could do on my own. I made decisions for myself and operated in my own best interest. As much as he thought he was putting me up on game, I hadn't been on the bench in a long time.

By the time I dropped my product off with Big Bang and Goose and made it back home, Darrel was in my driveway waiting for me.

"You ready, Slim? Let's get this party started," he told me. I backed the Range Rover up to the door inside of the garage and Darrel and I went inside. I had banded all of my cash together, wrapped blocks of bills together into one foot by one foot blocks with plastic wrap, and then wrapped them with gray electrical tape. Darrel had no idea what we were loading into the back of the Range Rover, and I'm sure he probably assumed they were blocks of cocaine. I had stacked all of the packages just inside of the garage door with several black duffel bags containing all of my jewelry and important paperwork and sealed with electrical tape underneath the zipper and zip ties connecting the two zippers on top of the stack.

Darrel and I packed the back seat and trunk of the Range Rover tightly with as many of the packages as we could fit inside, and then Darrel followed me to Dakota's house, trailing closely behind me with an AK-47 on his front seat. Dakota was sitting on the porch waiting for me to pull up, the tractor trailer parked on the street in front of her house. I hopped out of the Range Rover, hopped into the passenger seat of Darrel's car without a word, and returned home. Darrel and I packed the remaining packages and the duffel bags into the Porsche and took it over to Dakota's as well.

Darrel took me back home, watched me go inside and lock the door, and then pulled off. I immediately went down into the Drug Lair, pulled out my last two empty duffel bags, and sat them on the table. I released a deep sigh as I entered the combination on the safe and opened it. It was nearly empty with all of the money gone. I grabbed the last of the money and all of the guns- the .40, a .38, a .45, a .357, a .22, and a 9mm- and dropped them all into the first bag, along with all of the ammunition I had on hand to accompany the weapons.

Then I climbed the stairs to my room and gathered several pairs of jeans, t-shirts, a pant suit, a designer dress, tennis shoes, sandals, and a pair of Jimmy Choos. I picked out seven pairs of underwear and matching bras, two pairs of socks, and my La Perla set. Then I looked underneath my bathroom sink and grabbed my emergency toiletry bag that held a brand new toothbrush, tube of toothpaste, comb and brush, lotion, shower gel, and hand sanitizer, as well as a small bottle of alcohol and bandages. I dropped it all into the second duffel bag.

I knew I had to be ready to leave at any moment, so I loaded the duffel bags into the trunk of the Audi and placed my keys, my phones, and my second .45 on my nightstand. Then it hit me. My letters. I rushed into the office and unlocked the drawer hidden within the bottom right drawer. The envelope that held Curtis' letters was its only contents. I grabbed it and pressed it to my chest, closed my eyes and exhaled deeply. I went out to the garage and put the envelope in the bag with the guns and money, and on top, I dropped a picture of me and Curtis.

Chapter 19

Two days later, Max came banging at my door at seven in the morning. I already knew what it was before his lips parted to speak.

"Shonna, we have to go and we have to go right now. Pack up everything you want to take with you and come on," he said as he frantically snatched open my dresser drawers, only to find them empty.

"What's wrong, Max?" I sighed.

"Shonna, turn on the news. They've released a photo from the surveillance cameras at the front desk of the motel. They have a picture of you when you checked in. We have to go, Shonna. It's just a matter of time now," he said. My heart dropped into my kneecaps and then began to race. I felt two seconds of intense panic, and then, a sudden complete calmness. "Where are your clothes?" he asked me as he searched my dresser and chest and found them empty.

"Are you packed?" I asked him.

"Yes, baby. We have to go now. Right now."

"I'm going to get in the shower and get dressed. I want you to get on I-40 and go across the river to Southland Greyhound Park. Play the quarter slots and wait for me there. I will come find you," I instructed him calmly. Max frowned at me with a look that hinted disgust as well.

"Are you crazy? What are you talking about? We have to get as far away from here as soon as possible. We don't have time-"

"Shut up," I said sternly. "I have a plan. I am packed and ready. I just need to get dressed. If you're running with me, then you follow my instructions and try not to do anything stupid, like get yourself caught or killed," I told him. I stepped two inches away from his face and said with an eerie calmness, "And yes, I am crazy."

"Aight, Slim. Aight. I'll be at Southland waiting for you," he said as he backed up with his hands in the air. He kissed me on the cheek, told me to hurry, be careful, and that he loved me. With that, he left.

I rushed into the bathroom and hopped into the shower. The hot water lulled my mind and allowed me to think. I had tied up all of my loose ends. My clothing, shoes, photos, and all of my other valuables had been boxed and shipped to the house in Arizona the day before. My cars and excess money were en route to Arizona as well. Max had no clue that I already had an escape plan, or that I had already handled all of my own affairs. Max was a criminal mastermind, but he was neither a criminal nor a mastermind, at least not on the scale on which I was trying to exist.

When I got out of the shower, I got dressed, took one final walk-through of the beautiful home Curtis had built for us, set all of the alarms and the gate, locked up the house, got into the Audi, and left my home.

I stopped at a hobby store and picked up a ridiculous

amount of fake flowers. I had never been to my husband's grave, but I knew I couldn't leave without saying goodbye. I had always known exactly where he was buried, so I knew exactly where to find him. I pulled onto the road next to the section where Curtis was resting and grabbed my bag of faux roses, lilies, tulips, and chrysanthemums. Walking down the pathway towards the grave, each step grew heavier than the one before as somberness took over my entire body. I stopped and faced his headstone, and I stood there frozen in time. It was the most piercingly bitter slice of reality I had ever tasted. There was his name, his birth date, and underneath, his death date.

Suddenly, it hit me: this was real. Curtis and I hadn't broken up; we weren't separated or divorced, or even on a hiatus. Curtis had died. He was killed…in front of me, no less. He was not coming back. This was permanent and irreversible. There was no getting back together or reconciliation. He was never going to call me asking to come back home, telling me how much he loved and missed me, and confessing how stupid he had been for leaving me. Curtis had been in love with me since the moment he first saw me, and he had died just as equally in love, obsessed, and infatuated with me. The last words he spoke were a reminder of his love for me. As unconditional and undying as our love had always been, our relationship had come to an abrupt and tragic end the day his life had been taken, and there was nothing I could do about it. He would never come home to me again. It was over.

My heart couldn't take it. I dropped to my knees, tears pouring down my cheeks. My man, my man, my man, my man, I kept repeating in my mind. My mother fucking husband! I screamed out in agony, not giving one singular fuck who heard me or what they thought of me.

"Curtis!" I cried. "Curtis, please, baby! Oh, Curtis! God, no!" I looked down at my French manicure covering the lettering on the headstone. TAYLOR. My husband. He had made me a part of him, and now we were separated into two again. They took him from me and buried my heart six feet deep with him in his grave. I sobbed uncontrollably for my love. He had been my everything, and now I was left with nothing.

Curtis had no flowers and his grave had been untouched. As I cried, I slowly grabbed one flower at a time and stuck their stems down into the earth in front of the headstone. Curtis had a large family. The fact that none of them had placed even one flower on Curtis' grave was offensive to me. Here my husband was looking all unloved and that couldn't have been further from the truth. If no one else loved him, I did. If no one else missed him, I did. If no one else had been out there to visit him, I had.

I promised myself that when all of my chaos died down, I would come back to visit Curtis again. I couldn't leave him out there by himself. If his spirit was anywhere nearby, I certainly didn't want him to feel alone and unloved. No matter how far I went, I would always come back to my lost love.

As I planted the last flower, I ran my fingers over his name one last time, whispered, "Happy birthday, My Love," and walked back to my car.

*   ~   *   ~   *

Casinos never close. This, along with the fact that they were always crowded, made them the perfect emergency meeting place, especially for people who know how to blend in. I approached Max from the rear on the second floor of the casino as he sat at a slot machine but was almost completely consumed with the black jack table next to him. He was so engulfed that he didn't even notice me as I approached him.

"Hey, baby," I whispered in his ear as I kissed his cheek.

"Baby, come here," he said as he pulled my arm. I sat down at the machine next to him.

"What?"

"Watch this," he said. "I'm always right. I can tell you what card the dealer is going to draw next. Watch," he said eagerly.

I watched as the dealer dealt the middle-aged, middle class man an ace and a deuce and himself an eight and a nine. I looked at Max.

"A five or another deuce," he whispered. "That's what he's going to deal. Watch," he told me.

We watched as the player asked for a hit and the dealer flipped over a five. I slowly turned my head to look at Max who was staring intensely at the side of my head. He raised an eyebrow at me. Turning back to the game, the dealer had just flipped over his own cards- a King and a three- while the player was studying the Jack and deuce in front of him. He requested the assumed hit and I looked at Max who mouthed the words 'four, seven and five.' I looked back at the game and saw the four lying on the table as the dealer flipped over a seven. The player requested another hit and was dealt a five. I nearly screamed.

"How do you do that?" I whispered to Max as I sat down at the machine next to him.

"I don't know," he said as he shook his head bewildered.

"What do you mean? How do you know what's going to be dealt next?" I questioned him.

"It's like a mathematical deduction. It's like my mind runs a series of equations and deduces the most mathematically correct and logical answer all within a split second," he explained.

"What the hell?" I said under my breath. "Go play," I told him after thinking for a second. He looked at me like I had lost my mind. "I'm serious. Go over to the table and have a seat."

"Slim, we don't have time-"

"We really don't, but I want to see this shit in action. Just play a couple of hands," I told him. Max joined the game and won a thousand dollars with three hands, and then I made him get up. "C'mon. Let's go," I whispered to him. His newly discovered talent couldn't have revealed itself at a better time.

"Slim, where are we going? What are we going to do?" he asked me as we approached my car on the parking lot.

"Have you gassed up?" I asked him as I unlocked my doors.

"Yeah, I have a full tank. But what's up?"

"Get in," I told him. He got into the passenger seat of my car and stared at me. "We're going to Vegas," I told him.

"Vegas?" he frowned. "Why Vegas?"

"I've had this mapped out for months, but I never thought I'd actually have to use it. This thing you do with the cards, though, it could make us a lot of money. We're going to Vegas because it's far away from here, and it's crowded, so we can lay low there."

"That's what's up. You ready?" he asked hastily.

"What? No objection? No argument?" I asked shocked.

"Nah, Lil Momma. We gotta go. We can't stay here. I didn't think you had any kind of plan, but I knew we'd have to hit the road anyway. Let's get it. You ready to roll?"

"Yeah," I nodded, still wondering who this man was. "Yeah, let's go."

Max hopped into his own car and we hit the road. We only stopped for gas along the way until it got dark. We found a nice hotel, and Max paid cash for a suite. I was exhausted from the long, boring drive by myself, but I couldn't resist the tub calling my name. When I came out of the bathroom, I discovered Max had ordered room service for us. He had eaten his half of the boneless wings and pepperoni pizza and left the rest for me, along with a strawberry milkshake with whipped cream and a cherry on top.

I told myself at that moment as I watched Max grab a clean pair of boxers and go into the bathroom for his shower that he may have been a cheater and slick abusive, but at least he gave a fuck and at least he learned his lesson. I hadn't caught Max with any more women, but that hadn't stopped me from fucking Eric occasionally on nights when Max couldn't or wouldn't come through. Something about this moment, though, made me feel bad that I didn't care nearly as much about him as he cared about me. We had been together for months, but I had never given him my all. I had always looked at him like a friend with benefits who I was very close to, but he had never and probably would never capture my heart like Curtis had. I didn't really expect him to, and just thinking about it, I probably wouldn't have allowed him to. Besides, I didn't have much of a heart left anyway.

I ate and watched TV while Max showered, and when he came to bed, I cuddled underneath him and fell asleep.

It was almost midnight the next night when we made it onto the strip in Las Vegas. I pulled up at the first hotel that caught my eye- Caesar's Palace- and parked in front of the door. I got a normal room for the two of us with a fake ID and we valeted the cars for the night.

Chapter 20

Max and I were double trouble in Las Vegas. We had both tossed our "business phones" out of the cars in the middle of the highway in Oklahoma somewhere, so we knew no one would be able to track us. Max would count cards at the tables at the different casinos all day, and at night, I would meet up with guys at the bar, go back to their rooms, rob them of all cash, cards, and chips in their possession, and then come back to the room thousands of dollars richer. While Max was gone during the day, I was busy keeping my affairs in order back in Memphis and keeping up with things that were happening in Arizona.

My cars and belongings had all arrived in Arizona. The longer Max and I stayed in Las Vegas, the more money I packaged and shipped to my future home. I had also recovered the contents of the safe deposit box Curtis had in Las Vegas and sent the money and jewelry to the house with the rest of the money. One thing that I had noticed was that every box contained some sort of paperwork or documentation, and this one was no different. It held the titles to two cars- a Maserati Quattroporte GTS and an Aston Martin DB11– and three small black books that I discovered were the account ledgers for the off-shore accounts I had found the codes to months ago. Curtis had been stowing the bulk of his money in these accounts to keep himself under the already low-flying radar of the American government.

Curtis had to have been a fucking genius. His system had been flawless. He had not only hidden a few million dollars from the government and law enforcement authorities, but he had also hidden the entire operation from me. Curtis had been equally as considerate as inconsiderate, I told myself as I sat staring at our photograph one morning while Max was gone to The Mirage.

I understood why Curtis didn't tell me about what he was doing. I probably would've freaked out, and I know he didn't want me to think any less of him. My knowledge of the situation would've put me in danger as well. However, my ignorance of the situation had not assisted me in any way either. At the same time, for my husband to be in a tax bracket completely unheard of in our neighborhood- legal or not- and for us to be renting the miniscule little house in the hood was an insult to me. I was driving a car that had more health issues than my grandmother and working an inhumane number of hours at a job that only paid enough over minimum wage to be considered a 'good job' by fast food workers.

I, in my opinion, had been a great wife to my husband. I had given him everything he had ever asked of me except children, though we had been trying to get pregnant and Curtis had not faulted me for the lack of results. I cooked without him asking me to. I made every birthday extra special, and I was both loyal and faithful. Life back then had been simple, but it was hard. We were struggling to stay afloat, or so I thought, and every single paycheck mattered. I may not have been the best wife ever, but I certainly was not the worst. Either way, I didn't deserve to live under those conditions when my husband was essentially an underground King Pin.

I kept telling myself that Curtis had a number of reasons for hiding his entire lifestyle from me which caused him to hide his wealth as well. It was obvious, though, that he did it all solely for me to be able to live a better life after he was gone. It was also quite evident that he knew that day would come as well. I kept telling myself all of these things and still found myself angry at Curtis for having so much and divulging so little. I didn't deserve this life I was living now. If I was going to have it all, I felt like I should have had it all with the man I loved, adored, and married- my husband Curtis.

Max came in the room that afternoon and I was dressed to head out. He thought I was heading to the casino floor to recruit new victims, but I was headed to the airport to catch my flight to Seattle. I still had a list of boxes I had to recover the contents of, and being in the mid-west just made it that much easier to reach the boxes on that side of the country without being gone long enough to be missed. While in Memphis, I had recovered the safe deposit boxes in Chicago, St. Louis, Miami, Atlanta, Kansas City, and Dallas. I had already recovered the box in Las Vegas, and I had Los Angeles, Seattle, and Reno left.

I kissed him gently as I left out the door, smiled as I looked back while closing the door, and glanced down at my Jimmy Choos as I waited for the elevator. I caught a cab to the airport, made it to Seattle on time, emptied the box, mailed its contents, and made it back to Las Vegas in enough time to be sipping a Sex on the Beach at the bar at Treasure Island when Max stumbled upon me.

"There you are, baby," he said as he sat next to me and ordered a Jack and Coke. "It's rare that we ever cross paths while we're out, but it's always a pleasure."

"This is true," I nodded and smiled.

"I'm not sure why, but, baby, I've missed you today. I didn't want to bother you, so I didn't call or text, but I just had the undeniable urge to wrap my arms around you and hold you close tonight," he admitted.

"Really?" I raised an eyebrow. "You do realize this has become a sort of trend, don't you?"

"What do you mean?"

"Well, it's like you said: we rarely run into each other in the casinos, but when we do, it's almost always when we're missing each other."

"That's true," he said as he thought to himself. "It's that connection we have."

"Maybe," I told him. "Are you ready to go back to the room?"

"Actually, we're here now. I felt like we had been at The Venetian too long, so I moved us here."

"Here? When? When were you going to tell me?"

"Calm down, calm down," he said as he rubbed my arm. "I just checked us in just now. I was going to shoot you a text while I was at the bar, but I just happened that you're sitting here."

"Now, what if I was on my way to the room to get something or lay down? That would've been such a shock."

"Well, you weren't, so it worked out fine, so stop fussing."

"Whatever," I giggled.

"So, are you ready to go back to the room? We've been on this paper chase so long, it's been a minute, and I need some lovin'."

"You need some lovin', baby?" I teased. "Hell, I could use some too, honestly."

"Well, c'mon, sweet thang. Let's go. Let Daddy take care of you," he said as he offered me his hand.

I showered when we made it to the room, and Max took his turn after me. I lay across the bed watching TV while he was in the bathroom and dozed off unintentionally.

I woke up to Max rubbing my thighs and massaging my ass cheeks. I moved back against his dick and began to grind against it as I felt his hand move it into position and rub it back and forth in my wetness until it slipped inside. I sighed, and he placed warm kisses on the back of my neck as his sweet breath blew in my hair. He wrapped his arms around my body and held me close as he stroked me slowly, deeply, hitting my spot. He placed his face in the curve my neck and inhaled my essence, and I lost my breath at just the tingle.

My hand reached back and caressed his cheek as I turned my face and our lips met. My moans trickled from my lips onto his as he slid my leg up to bend and then palmed by breasts. My breathing grew heavier with each stroke; my temperature rose with each grind. Max slid my leg back down and pushed my hip forward as he sat up to stroke me even deeper, and I cried out in ecstasy as he struck a chord within my body that felt like the sweetest melody. It was the softness of Sevyn Streeter and the intensity of Whitney Houston all wrapped into each thrust.

Max's fingertips found their way around my neck and I frowned at the fact that I liked it. He squeezed just tightly enough to grip but not choke me. I could feel the wind as it flowed between us as he pumped more rapidly, the sweat-moistened skin of his pelvis sounding off as it slapped the flesh on the curve of my ass. The cold air alternating with the fire of our body heat set my hormones ablaze. Wide awake, I pushed Max back onto the bed and slid down on his pole.

Max released an incredible sigh of relief as he reentered me. I bounced on his dick, rolling my hips and grinding down hard on it. Max sat up while I was still on it, swung his legs over the edge of the bed, and leaned me back as he slammed my pussy down on his dick my lifting me by my hips. I held onto his biceps as he pumped, closing my eyes so that I could zone out.

Suddenly, Max stood up, turned around, and laid me on the bed. Moving me to the edge, he spread my legs wide and held my hips as he pumped into me. My moans echoed inside of my own head. Even my thoughts were screams of pure pleasure. I ran my fingers over Max's chiseled and tattooed chest down to his abs, noting how unbelievably sexy he had always been to me. I watched him watching his dick run in and out of my womb. I surveyed his face, noticing the little mole here, the dark spot there. He really was a beautiful man. I had never really watched Max's face as we made love, but this time was different.

The corner of his lips began to turn upward in a twitch and his muscles flexed. His chest jumped and one of his eyebrows raised. He wasn't looking up at me anymore. He was focused on his dick sliding in and out of my wetness. His lips formed an "O" and I lay there taking in the entire series of facial expressions. It was incredible. Max grunted deeply as his eyes closed and his head leaned back. He was feeling it. I was feeling it too, but I was so caught up watching Max that it distracted me from the pleasure my own body was experiencing. I had stopped moaning; I had stopped moving and reacting all together. I was just lying there watching, observing.

Max's eyes opened and stared at the ceiling as he pumped and then he looked straight back down to where we met at the center. He grunted again and then again and his hands squeezed my hips tightly. My womb suddenly became flooded with heat as he shot his man milk deep inside of me. I was satisfied. The most satisfying feeling was knowing I could send him to the highest peak of an orgasm possible. Just knowing that I could make him cum just did something to me. You see, men can't be satisfied by any woman, just like women can't be satisfied by just any man. Just like men, women are all made differently. What feels like heaven to one man may feel like a waste of time to another. To one man, a particular pussy may feel like sticking his dick out of an open window, while to another, it may feel like everything he's ever been looking for. So just knowing that my pussy made my man nut so hard that he was completely drained and he fell almost immediately asleep- which was the case at that moment- brought a sense of completion like no other.

So, I lay there staring at the ceiling, complete and or-gasm-less, while Max lay next to me snoring, unaware of his completion or incompletion with testicles completely drained and empty.

Chapter 21

"Slim, what the fuck is going on?!" Max said as he shot up in the bed. I had thrown the door open so hard that it smacked the door stopper when I entered the room. I was sweating, out of breath, and completely frantic. Max rose from the bed frowning at my chaos.

"Max, we have to go. We have to go now," I said as I threw my clothes into my duffel bag. Max approached me from behind, but I turned to him before he could grab me. "Now, Max! Get your stuff. We have to go."

"Shonna, tell me what the fuck is going on!"

"Does it look like I have time to explain shit to you?" I yelled. "Why do you always need an explanation? Get your shit, Max! We have to get the fuck out of here now!" I was frustrated to my wits' end and stood there staring at him. He read the seriousness in my eyes and then began grabbing his belongings too. I rushed into the bathroom and grabbed my shower gels, toothbrush, razors, everything that I had dropped there, sat here, misplaced there. I opened the little safe in the closet and pushed all of the money Max and I had stashed there into my bag with one motion. When I turned around, Max was stepping into his jeans, his shirt unbuttoned and hanging from his shoulders.

"Shonna-"

"Shut up, Max," I growled.

"Shonna-"

"Shut the fuck up and let's go!" I yelled again. "Shit!"

"Shonna, fucking talk to me!" he said as he grabbed my arm and snatched me backwards.

"Max, either you're coming with me or you're staying. All I know is if you hold me back for even one more second, so help me God, I'll shoot your mother fucking ass too. Now get your fucking hands off of me," I said with a low, eerie calmness. Max released my arm and stared straight into my eyes.

"Go ahead. Leave. But I'm not coming with you," he said. I stared at him for a second too long. I guess he thought I was feeling disbelief, shock, disappointment, sadness, even confusion. Honestly, I was slick relieved. Being without Max would mean one less person I was responsible for. It was like dropping your Louis Vuitton luggage at the front door when you make it home from a long trip. It was easier to hide just me, easier to be overlooked when you're only in one car. Max was a convenient inconvenience. I looked at him long and hard, challenging him with my eyes, and then turned and walked out the door.

* ~ * ~ *

I had been scouting at the bars all night, but hadn't found anyone who was worth my time. I was sitting there in my Chanel dress, clicking the heels of my Louboutins against the legs of the barstool when a handsome white guy no older than a college senior walked up and offered me a twin to the

Sex on the Beach I was nursing. He was wearing Ralph Lauren, not Polo, and he smelled of a cologne so delicious I could have licked him. He seemed innocent enough, so I accepted the drink. He ordered himself a drink as well as he made small talk and then invited me to a party in a suite. All I heard was more people, and more people meant more money.

The party was actually a very large group of his friends who had come to Vegas for a bachelor party. There was liquor everywhere, white boys completely wasted, and even a little bit of powder being passed around. So I lured one of the oldest ones off to a bedroom. He had been all flashy, bragging that he had paid for the room, the liquor, the drugs, and the food, so of course he was my primary target. I got his drunk ass all the way in that room and closed the door. I did a little dance for him and then pushed him back on the bed and straddled him. I unbuttoned my blouse as he unbuttoned and removed his own. I heard the light thud of him kicking off his shoes, and before I knew it, he was in his boxers, I was in my bra and panties, and we both were underneath the covers. He had whispered to me that he'd never been with a black woman before. I was amused. A voice in my head told him that truth be told, he wasn't going to be with one today either.

I blinked my long lashes at him as he moved closer to me. His hands began to roam as his lips carefully placed kisses wet with thick saliva all over my breasts, neck, and chest. I could smell the alcohol on his breath and seeping from his pores.

"You got a condom?" he asked as he came up from between my breasts.

"Yeah, of course," I said as I smiled. I reached down beside the bed and slipped my .22 out of its thigh holster. "I always carry protection," I said as I turned back around and pointed the gun at his nose, but he already had a .9 mm pointed at mine.

"You thought you were going to rob me, didn't you?" he grinned. "You've got another thing coming, bitch. You robbed my friend Joe last week," he revealed. "The guy with the blue sweat suit at Planet Hollywood?" he said to jog my memory. I knew exactly who he was talking about, but my face remained indifferent. "Anyway, you got a couple of G's off of him, and half of that was mine, so I'm going to need my money back… now," he said. I stared at him unimpressed and unmoved.

"I suggest you get this gun out of my face," I said calmly.

"I suggest you hand over my money."

"Let me tell you what's not going to happen," I said. "I'm not handing you anything, and neither are you going to take anything from me. What you are going to do is get that gun out of my face because you and I both know you are not a killer and you're not going to shoot me. And if I look down the barrel of this nine, and there's no bullet in the chamber, it's only going to piss me off," I said sweetly. "So you're going to hand over all of the cash you have on you. Then you're going to wait two minutes after I leave this room before you open the door."

"I'm not giving you anything! Are you crazy?" he

laughed. "You've lost your damn mind. Get up and go get the money out of your pockets," he ordered. When I didn't move, he cocked the gun.

POW!

Blood splattered across the pillows as he lifeless body fell back. I had done it again. I sat there in shock for a few seconds until the door burst open and one of his drunken friends yelled, "What the fuck?!" He reached for his waist, and I shot him too. I was on my knees in the bed now, as several other men came running to the door and I dropped them one by one, counting my shots in my head. My gun ran out of bullets, but I wasn't close enough to my purse to get my extra magazine, so I snatched the gun from their dead friend on the bed.

I jumped up, clothed in nothing but a black lace Victoria's Secret thong and matching lace-back bra. I had to get out of there. I grabbed my shirt and jeans and tossed them onto the bed, the gun still aimed at the door. I had heard all of the women run out of the door when the shooting first started, so I knew I wouldn't have to blow any bitches' brains out. Two more guys came running to the door.

"Oh, my God! Oh, my God! What the fuck?" the first one yelled. He looked up at me standing there sexy as shit with a gun pointed at his face and for two seconds I saw the lust in his eyes…and then I shot him too.

I had a pile of men at the doorway and another guy stepping over them trying to get into the room. When he finally did, he was seriously trying to talk to me.

"Stop! Stop! Don't shoot!" he said with his hands in the air. "You don't have to do this!"

"Either get the fuck out of here or get shot too!" I told him.

"No," he shook his head. "I'm not going to run, and you're not going to shoot me. Put the gun down," he said as he started to approach me.

"Yo, I'm not putting no mother fucking gun down, so stop right there where you at or I'm popping your ass Too just like the rest of your weak ass home boys who done ran in here trying to save this one nigga who is already dead as hell," I told him.

"You're too beautiful for this shit," he shook his head and said. "You don't want to do this."

"Yeah, well, beauty hurts," I told him.

In a group, there's always one. Somebody always has to be the damn negotiator. They always like to play good cop, bad cop. You shoot up all of the bad cops and then here comes this one little good cop trying to make it all right. At the end of the day, though... they're all cops.

POW!

There was no more movement in the room. I threw on my jeans and blouse and went to each body and took their whole wallets. I didn't care about the police being able to identify the bodies or notify the families. I just grabbed the whole wallets and any loose money in their pockets and tossed it all into my purse. I knew that security was probably on their way up, so I peeked out of the bedroom, stepped into my Louboutins, and went straight to the table where the women had been dancing. I scooped up all of the money, tossed it into my purse, and then darted out the door at full speed.

I jumped into the open elevator and took it down three floors, thinking the entire time that this would've never happened if I had worn my Jimmy Choos. My Jimmy Choos were like my good luck charms; nothing ever went wrong when I wore them. I had been trying to be cute and trendy when I threw on the Louboutins, and I could run in any heel, no matter the brand, but I had Jimmy Choo feet. I could run in them like they were Nike Air Max's. I got off the elevator and ran to the stairs and down seven flights. Then I got back on the elevator and took it down to the second floor and then took the stairs to the first floor and ran out a side door straight to my car, which was parked on the lot belonging to the casino next door. Flinging my door open, I tossed my purse onto the passenger seat, and flew out of the parking lot onto the street without even looking for oncoming traffic.

"Shit! Shit! Shit!" I screamed as my fists pounded the steering wheel. "Fuuuuuuuuck!!!"

I had no clue if Max was in our hotel room, but I told myself if he wasn't I was going to grab all of his belongings with mine and call him to tell him where to meet me. I slid my car into valet and ran through the door to the elevator. The whole time, I was just praying I didn't get caught. I was praying even harder, though, that Max didn't get caught with me. He didn't deserve to be locked up for the foul shit I had done. I didn't care that I had killed that police officer to protect him. He didn't owe me anything for that. I didn't care that he had betrayed my trust by cheating on me. I had already gotten my revenge for that shit. I didn't know all of the wrongdoing Max had possibly done in his life, but I just knew I wasn't going to allow him to endure one day of jail time because of my ill deeds. It was mine, and if the time came, I would own up to it. But at that moment, I wasn't trying to do any jail time. All I gave a fuck about was getting up to that room and getting away.

Chapter 22

I slammed my trunk closed and Max was standing there, his bags thrown over his shoulder. Our eyes connected in a silent understanding. I saw something more in his gaze, though, but I couldn't quite place it. I could have called it love, but it was a completely different kind of love. It was something all too familiar, and yet, still so foreign. I told him to meet me at Caesar's Palace. He nodded and headed towards his car. I watched him from behind as he walked away, shaking my head.

I drove down to Caesar's Palace and parked at the back of the lot. Max whipped up right behind me and parked next to me facing the opposite direction so that our driver's side windows were facing each other.

"We've got to gas up," I told him. "Road trip."

"Following you," he nodded and said simply.

After filling our tanks, I hit the road headed to Arizona. I clipped my phone into its holder, connected it to my in-car system with the Bluetooth, and called Max.

"What's up?" he answered.

"I'm sorry for yelling at you back there."

"It's all good. I'm good."

"And thank you for coming with me," I offered.

"We're in this shit together, Slim. No matter what, I got your back," he assured me. "I promised I'd take care of you, and I'm going to do just that."

"You don't have to take care of me, Max. I'm grown. I can take care of myself."

"It's not about you being grown. Everybody needs somebody they can depend on. You aren't alone, Shonna. I have your back, even if it's just as your backup. I got you."

"Well, either way, thank you."

"You're welcome. So, where are we going?"

"We're going to Phoenix, Arizona," I told him.

"Phoenix? Why?"

"I've got a house there we can crash at for a while," I told him.

"You've got a house in Phoenix?" he asked in disbelief.

"Yeah, and that's where we're going."

"So what happened? Why are we vacating Vegas so impromptu?"

"Well," I sighed deeply. "I just killed a whole group of white guys in a suite."

"What? What happened, Slim?" His concern was evident in his voice.

"I was having a slow night. I was sitting at the bar, and a guy walked up and bought me a drink. We were talking and he invited me to this party in a suite, so of course I went. You know I'm always about the move. It was a prime opportunity," I explained.

"Okay. So what happened?"

"I got up there, scoped out the big baller- because you know I don't play with the do-boys and the minions,- and I got him to go off to one of the bedrooms with me. I got him going and set him up for the jack move, and he pulled a pistol on me. He said I robbed one of his friends last week and he had been watching me. He was just trying to get his money back, but you know I wasn't going. I have a strict no refund policy. He cocked his gun, and I shot his ass right there in the bed."

"Damn, Slim. So then let me guess. All of his friends came in there when they heard the gun shot?"

"You already know it. Man, those niggas were coming around that corner like I was playing The Walking Dead or Gears of War on the Xbox. I used all of my bullets and his too. I had a pile of white boys at the bedroom door like on Django. They just kept coming like they didn't see the ten mother fuckers before them laying there with their noodles knocked out. Then the last one acted like he was supposed to be a damn negotiator and was trying to get me to put the gun down like I was on the ledge or something. I offed his ass too."

"Damn, Slim! You used two magazines of bullets? One bullet per person?"

"Yep."

"Damn! So you offed about twenty people!" I could tell by his tone that he was impressed.

"Umm, yeah. Give or take," I confirmed.

"Shit, Slim! Are you okay?"

"I think so. I just can't believe that shit just happened."

"I know. Well, look. When you're ready to stop for the night, you just pull up somewhere. I'm following you."

"Bet."

Any other time, a trip from Las Vegas to Phoenix would have been a non-stop trip. But Max knew that I had already been up all night and it was nearing time for me to tap out. I did a lot of thinking while I drove. I was glad I had already gotten around to the rest of the safe deposit boxes. It was one less thing I had to worry about. I had a half dozen duffel bags in my trunk, and I knew I must've had hella shit waiting for me at the house. Luckily for me, I had come to realize that Curtis had a house sitter on the payroll who went by the house weekly to retrieve packages and keep the property maintained.

My mind did a double take at the thought of Curtis. Sometimes I believed it was nothing but the flashbacks and memories that got me through. I remembered the night Curtis died. He was lying there, sleeping so peacefully. I had watched him sleep for a moment, caught up in how incredibly handsome he was to me. I was extra careful when I got out of the bed, not wanting to wake him. And yet, he was still awakened, and in the worst way possible.

All of that time I had spent with Curtis, I decided, I had not been blind. Everything he had been doing was meant to be kept from me. It was not meant for me to know. There was no room for my opinions or understanding. I still didn't fully understand and probably never would, but nevertheless, I was grateful. Curtis had kept me out of harm's way and prevented me from becoming an accessory in his activities.

Everything that had occurred since Curtis passed was a direct result of my own decisions. I didn't have to start selling drugs. I could have destroyed them or just dumped them. I didn't have to start robbing people and I didn't have to kill people. All of that was of my own doing, and if I knew my husband and his intentions, I knew that he was probably upside down in his grave because of my behavior.

As horrible as it sounded, though, I loved what I was doing. I had a particular knack for masterminding and performing criminal activity. Just about everything I had done thus far had been with precision, and the few things that had gone wrong- as extreme as they were- had been handled with such professionalism that they couldn't even be called mishaps. They were simply occurrences or situations. However, my own morale, I realized, had severely deteriorated, and my deeds had progressed from bad to worse. But for some reason, I couldn't see myself any differently. Not without preventing my husband's death which set forth the series of catastrophic criminal events.

Still driving in the open darkness of the Arizona desert, my mind wandered back to the place where I had awoken first. It had been a number of months, almost a year. Lil Don and Glenn were decomposed beyond recognition by now, if there was anything left of them at all after the rats and whatever local insects had had their fill of them. I had to admit: I did that. That situation was set up for my death without even a chance of escape, and instead, I had turned the entire scenario around. I had killed my captors and robbed them of the very same fortune they were looking to steal from me. Did I have any regrets? Only that I hadn't tortured them longer and made them suffer more. But I resolved that I had done more than enough, especially given the extreme circumstances.

My thoughts were interrupted by my phone ringing. It was the middle of the night, so when my screen read MOM, I was apprehensive about answering. Nevertheless, I picked up and was immediately concerned.

"Shonna," she said with tears in her voice.

"Hey, Mom. What are you doing up so late? It's 2:30 where I am, so I know it's half past midnight there. What's wrong?"

"Shonna, sweetie, it's Dakota," she whimpered.

"What do you mean? What's wrong with Dakota?" I

asked. My heart was banging against the walls of my breast-bone.

"They.... They found her dead in a hotel room!" My mother began crying hysterically.

"Oh, my God! Mom, no! What happened?" I was in shock.

"They heard shots being fired in a hotel room out there by the penal farm, and someone saw a man running away from the room. The police got up there, and she was dead on the floor with a gun still in her hand," my mother told me between sniffles.

"Oh, momma, no! I said quietly. I couldn't believe what I was hearing.

"Oh, Shonna! I'm so sorry, baby," she cried. "I'm so sorry."

"Oh, God! No, Lord! Not Dakota!" I said quietly as I shook my head in utter disbelief. Not my best friend. Not Dakota. She had been my best friend as long as I could re-member. If I had no one else in my corner, I had always had Dakota. She just couldn't be gone.

"I'm sorry, baby. I have to go," my mother told me. "I need to go pull myself together."

I drove for about a half an hour as I let my mother's words sink in. My best friend was dead, found on the floor of a hotel room with a gun in her hand. She was trying to rob someone without a cover man. She was doing the same shit we had been doing, but she was doing it by herself and it cost her her life. My heart hurt. I had introduced Dakota to something that had led to her death.

After a few minutes, I just couldn't take it anymore. I was crying so hard I could barely see the road ahead of me. Throwing the door open, I got out, bent over with my hands on my knees, and let out a scream like none other I had ever heard come from within me.

"Slim! What's wrong?" Max yelled as he ran up to me.

"Dakota! They killed Dakota!" I screamed. He gasped. I dropped to my knees in emotional agony.

"No, baby! What the fuck happened?"

"They found her dead in a hotel room!" I sobbed. "It's all my fault! It's all my fault!"

"It's not your fault, baby. You can't blame yourself for this."

"Yes, it is! I should've never brought her into this with us. I got her started on this shit, and now she's dead! Oh, my God! They killed my best friend!"

"Shonna-"

"No! No!" I shook my head. "I should've been there. I should've been there to protect her. She needed me. She needed somebody there with her."

"Shonna," Max said quietly, "I know you wanted to be there and protect her, just like someone, anyone, should've been there to protect you. But, Shonna, you've got your own life to live, your own set of choices and decisions to make. You can't live your life taking care of everybody else. You've got to make the best decision you can for yourself before you think about everyone else. Look," he said as he raised my head with his thumb underneath my chin. "If you had stayed in Memphis, you'd be in the feds by now just getting started on a life sentence. You had to make the best move for you. I know losing Dakota is a hard pill to swallow, but, baby, that's life. Do you know what life really is?" I shook my head no. "This is what happens in life: You spend your whole life watching everybody around you that you love die. Your siblings, your parents, your friends, your grandparents, aunts, uncles, cousins- they're all going to die. And then you die too. That's the game of life, so you'd better live it while you're here because one day it'll be your turn, and that's one decision that we don't get to make."

I just looked at Max. As pessimistic and painful as what he had just said was, he had just spit some real knowledge. He was completely right, as much as I hated to admit it. It wasn't that I hated for Max to be right. I just hated that what he had just said was actually true. It seemed like it was just too fucked up to be real. Maybe it was just too fucked up NOT to be real.

Max reached out and offered his hand to me. "C'mon, baby. Let's go grab a room somewhere for a few hours. You need some rest. It's not safe out here on the side of the road in the middle of the night. You're going to get our asses eaten by some coyotes or something out here," he joked, but I knew he was serious. I grabbed his hand and he pulled me to my feet. "Just pull up at the first little motel you see off the side of the interstate and we'll crash there for the night," he told me.

I hopped back into my car, wiping tears and sniffling. I was tired. Tired of taking losses, tired of death, tired of taking two steps forward and three steps back. I had made thousands of dollars in Las Vegas, but all the money in the world couldn't replace that little white girl I had met in my sixth grade science class. I had been up in that damn suite knocking niggas' noodles out, and it felt like one of those bullets had caught my best friend. It felt like I had pulled the trigger and shot the bullet that killed her myself. As self-destructive as she had always been, ultimately, I had been the cause of her demise.

The next exit was in Wickenburg, and I spotted a small motel off the side of the interstate and pulled over. The place was so old, it still had a vacancy light, which was on. I had to ring the bell six times before the elderly white woman came around the corner.

"It's fifteen dollars an hour," she said without even looking at me.

"Umm, I kind of was looking for a nightly rate," I said quietly.

"Oh, sweetness, I'm sorry. It'll be thirty dollars a night," she said and broke into a series of hacking coughs that should've raised her lungs from the dead and skinned the lining of her esophagus.

"Okay, umm, I'll take one room for the night," I told her.

"Well, thirty bucks," she said. I slid her three tens through the slot in the window which she folded and stuck in her bra as she walked through a door and then out of the office into the open night air. "You don't look like anyone we've had here in a long time, dear, so I'm going to give you our cleanest room. Follow me."

I followed her directly across the parking lot to room nineteen, and she unlocked and opened the door and handed me the key. I flipped on the light and looked around.

"I know it's not what you're used to, but it's the best we've got," she said and I turned around and frowned at her. I had been expecting cigarette burns in the comforter, torn carpet, dingy drapes, a ring around the tub, and a TV with an antenna older than me on the back.

"This is one of your cleanest rooms?" I asked her.

"Well, you don't have to insult me. I know it's not a Clorox commercial, but you won't catch chlamydia from the sheets either," she put her hand on her hip and said.

"No, ma'am. It's… it's perfect. This is a great room," I told her. "Thank you. Thank you so much."

"Well, you're welcome, deary. Checkout is at eleven," she said as she headed out of the room. "The wi-fi password is on the back of the door, and if you need more towels, I have them at the front desk." She closed the door behind herself, and I turned on the flat screen that was mounted to the wall and sat on the edge of the bed. Five minutes later, there was a knock on the door.

"Max! Shit!" I whispered to myself as I jumped up to open the door.

"Care to invite me inside or must I sleep in the car like I'm the help?" he asked sarcastically.

"Get your butt in here," I said as I rolled my eyes at him.

"I'm saying though. You done cut the TV on and kicked off your shoes and got comfortable and didn't even bother to call me or send up a smoke signal or nothing. Lucky for me, I was paying attention, so I saw what room you went into. If I hadn't, I'd be stretched out in the driver's seat for the night."

"Really, Max? Stop being so melodramatic." I turned and went back to the bed and laid across it.

"Whatever," he chuckled. "You need me to grab anything out of the car for you?"

"Naw, I'll get it," I told him, thinking about all of the other bags in my trunk that Max didn't know about.

"Well, I'll come with you," he offered.

"No, I'm good. I'm just going to run out there and come on back."

"It's dangerous for you to be out there by yourself," he tried to tell me, but I wasn't having it.

"Max, I just walked across the parking lot with a woman who is old enough to be my grandmother and could in no way protect my life or even assist me in protecting hers if need be. As you can see, we were both unharmed during the event. Therefore, I believe I shall be fine without your assistance, especially given that I'm always equipped for quick and proper extermination of any pests."

Max just stared at me following my dissertation, shook his head, and then said, "Just go ahead, Slim. Ain't nobody got time for that bullshit." I laughed and went out to my car. When I returned, Max had changed into a pair of pajama pants and fallen asleep. I changed into a large t-shirt, cut off the lights, snuggled under Max, and fell asleep too.

Chapter 23

"Shonna, where are we going? We passed Phoenix thirty minutes ago." Max was on the phone trying to figure out what was going on.

"Just drive, Max. I've got the GPS going. We're almost there," I told him.

"So the house isn't in Phoenix then. We're miles past Phoenix now, Slim."

"No, it's not in Phoenix, but it's not far. Just drive, baby. I got this. Okay?"

"Aight, Slim."

I made the turn the phone instructed me to make and kept driving down a long and winding road until it came to a clearing that revealed a gated driveway. I pressed the button on the call box.

"May I help you?" came a female's voice.

"Alexander Graham Bell, Thomas Edison, and Henry Ford to see Ms. Maron," I said clearly.

"Yes, sir," the woman said. The gate buzzed and then opened, and I entered the gate with Max behind me. There was a long driveway lined by beautiful cactus flowers, shrub verbenas, and even jojoba. There were tall cacti and trees just off from the flowers, and it all created an enchanting desert forest atmosphere.

When the driveway opened up, I stopped the car in shock and awe. I must have the wrong place, I thought to myself, but then remembered that I had just used the correct code to get into the gate. I threw my door open and stepped out of the car with one hand on my hip and the other shielding my eyes from the sun. Max came up behind me and wrapped his arm around my waist.

"Shonna, is this the right house?" he asked in the same disbelief I was experiencing.

"Yes, it is. Yes, yes, it is," I said, trying to convince myself as well.

"Whose house is this, Slim?"

"Mine," I said as my hand flew up to cover my mouth and my voice cracked. "It's mine."

"Yours?" Max frowned. "How the hell-"

"I don't know. I don't know," I shook my head, "but it's mine. It belongs to me." We stood there just looking at the compound, and then I motioned for us to get back into the cars. "Come on," I told him. "Let's go."

The words "big," "huge," "large" didn't even begin to describe the house. It was colossal. It was a house the size of a castle. The physical building itself had to have sat on an acre of land. There were buildings behind and around the main house, though I had no clue what they were. I drove up to the front door with Max just behind me, and we were greeted by a beautiful black woman with very familiar eyes.

"You must be Shonna," the woman said as she rushed over to me.

"Yes, I am," I confirmed. The woman wrapped her arms around me and hugged me tightly.

"I'm so happy to finally meet you! I'm Jerri!" she introduced herself.

"Well, it's nice to meet you. Who are you?"

"I, umm, I know we've never met, but I'm Curtis' twin sister," she revealed.

"Curtis had a twin that I didn't know about?"

"Yes, and that twin would be me."

"I'm sorry," I shook my head confused. "You're twins, but your names don't match."

"Oh, but they do. Curtis is named after Curtis Mayfield, and I'm named after Jerry Butler, Jr. The two of us were melody and harmony in human form, frick and frat," she explained.

"Oh, my God," I said quietly. All of those years, no one in Curtis' family had ever said anything about Curtis having a twin sister, and yet, here she was standing in front of me with my husband's eyes, nose, and skin tone. "I've got so many questions, but right now just isn't the time. Do you live here?"

"I had been living here for a while, but I got my own place, so I just come by and check the mail and make sure the house is secure. It's never been broken into and it's actually very secure. It's hard to find. You'd really have to be lost to just stumble upon it," she said.

"Well, thank you so much for taking care of the house for me."

"Oh, it's no problem. Here are the keys and the remotes to the gates and garages. It's all yours."

"You're not leaving, are you?"

"Oh, honey, yes. I've got to get on back home. If you need me for anything, my number is on the fridge," she said. She hugged me and then hopped into her Mercedes and pulled off. Max got out of his car and walked up to me.

"So, it's all yours?"

"Yep, it's all mine," I nodded.

"Who was that chick?"

"She's Curtis' twin sister."

"For real? You didn't tell me Curtis had a twin."

"Hell, I didn't know."

"You just found out? Damn! That's rough," he shook his head. "C'mon. Let's go inside."

*   ~   *   ~   *

"Yeah, I've been doing real well. I want y'all to come out here for a couple of days so we can discuss business. Aight, cool. I sent y'all some plane tickets. They should be there tomorrow. Yeah, the flight is in three days. No, no, y'all don't need no money. I got y'all. No, seriously. I got y'all. Aight. I'll see you then."

I had only been in my new home a couple of days, but it was already back to business. Max and I had already explored the mansion's eight bedrooms, twelve bathrooms, living room, game room, chef's kitchen, office and bunker. One of the large buildings behind the house was actually a showroom sized garage that held not only the cars that I had shipped to the house, but all of the other cars I had found titles for in the safe deposit boxes. Max began parking his car inside as well and was even considering having his cars shipped there too.

"I miss my Beamer," he had told me the night before. "I had just had those nice ass Daytons put on it. It was sitting up high on those sixes looking sexy as shit." So I told him to call and make the arrangements and we'd make sure we got the Beamer and the Challenger out there.

I had left Memphis months ago. I felt like all of my loose ends should have been tied up. But they weren't. I had the combination to the stand-up safe that Curtis had in the office. It had been in the safe deposit box in Los Angeles. Inside of the safe, on top of all of the money and jewelry, I found ledgers and a book of phone numbers. Along with Big Bang, Darrel, and Goose, even Lil Don and Glenn, I found a number for a man named Luchesi. He ran a professional cleaning service. The house didn't need a professional cleaning service. It was spic and span from the roof to the bunker. I found it suspicious, so I called the number.

Luchesi had been expecting my call. He had heard about Curtis' death and knew that inevitably I would have an inquiring mind. He explained to me that the services his company rendered were not of maid caliber. His company professionally disposed of corpses and cleaned execution scenes. Luchesi had been Curtis' cleaner of choice and Curtis had been known to set up appointments prior to killing someone and even flying Luchesi's staff across the country to clean unexpected or unintended sites. His services were expensive, of course, but more than worth it. The chemicals he used removed all signs of blood and bodily fluid so well that even a forensics expert would come up empty-handed.

Two days later, the doorbell rang. Big Bang. Goose. I smiled. I opened the door in my navy blue khaki dress and cute little Jimmy Choo heels, make-up and hair on point. They smiled widely and hugged me as they entered the house.

"Oowwee! Slim, you're living large out here!" Big Bang said as he looked around. "This is a helluva house!"

"Hell yeah, Slim. I ain't seen no shit like this nowhere in Memphis," Goose said in his usual cool, calm demeanor.

"Y'all follow me to my office," I said and then led them down the hallway.

"Yo, you want me to close the door?" Goose asked as I sat down behind the desk.

"Nah. Ain't nobody here but us. We're good."

"So why did you call us here?" Big Bang asked as he got comfortable in the chair in front of my desk.

"Well, first let me give you this," I said as I handed them each a bundle of hundreds.

"Damn, Slim. That's what's up. Good looking out," Big Bang said.

"Well, I told you that you didn't need any money and that I'd take care of y'all, and I always make good on my promises, so there you have it," I said simply. "So, gentlemen, I felt like I was due a report on the progress on my investment," I said as I folded my hands in my lap, secretly fingering the handle of the .45 that was secured underneath the desk.

"Well, you should have told us. We would've prepared an official report," Big Bang laughed.

"There's no need for any paperwork or charts," I said. "I just need an update is all."

"I mean, what you wanna know, Slim?" Goose asked me.

"What do you mean, Goose? I want to know where the fuck my damn money is. That's what I want to know."

"What do you-"

"How much of my product have you sold?" I cut him off.

"We've only got about a quarter of it left, but-"

"So you've sold over half of the shit I brought you? I've been gone what? Five months? Something like that? Why haven't I seen any return on my investment?" I looked at the two of them.

"Slim, I-"

"Nah, nah, Goose." I shook my head. "Bang, haven't we already had this problem?"

"Yeah, we have," he responded.

"I mean, this all seems vaguely familiar," I told him. "It's becoming a bit redundant, don't you think?"

"I believe so," he nodded nervously. I could see the shame in his face.

"We've already had a discussion about my money before, so why are we having it again? Why am I talking to you about this again, Bang?"

"It's my bad, Slim. I mean-"

"You're damned right it's your bad because you assured me yourself that we would not have this issue. You assured me that this conversation would not take place. But you know what? Maybe it's my bad. My bad for believing you. You know what they say. Fool me once, shame on you. Food me twice, shame on me. Maybe I should've never trusted you after that first incident." I raised an eyebrow at Bang.

"Naw, Slim. You can trust us-"

"I'm not talking about us and we and y'all. I'm talking about you. I can't write your resume based on Goose's qualifications. You tow may be a team, but a team is only as strong at the character of the individuals that compose it." I searched his eyes to be sure he understood me, and then I turned my attention to Goose. "Goose, we've always had a very professional relationship. We've never had any kind of misunderstandings or discrepancies. So you should understand why I told you to a slightly higher regard and why I actually expect a real answer from you." Goose nodded. "What happened, Goose."

"I honestly don't have a complete answer for that, Slim. I can only account for my own actions."

"I only expect you to account for your own for your own actions. Bang is a full grown adult. He should be able to account for his actions as well," I told him.

"For the most part, Slim, I was the one serving your product. I kept all of the money at Bang's house. I had an envelope labeled "Profit" and an envelope labeled "Slim." I'd put the money in the two envelopes and occasionally I'd pull from the "Profit" envelope. If I was in a rush, I'd just hand the money to Bang to put in the envelopes. Every other month, Bang would take the money out of the envelope to send to you, and that's what we've been doing the past few months."

"So Bang was supposed to send me the money?"

"I mean, of course, it was both of our responsibility, but that was the arrangement he and I had, so that's what I thought he was doing. I had no clue that he hadn't until just now, and that's what I was trying to tell you."

"So, Bang, what happened to my money?"

"What do you mean? I mean, shit, I spent it." He shrugged his shoulders. "Bills came up. I needed some things. I ended up spending it," he said simply.

"And that's okay? It's fine for you to do that?" I asked him.

"I'm not saying that it's okay, but it's what happened."

"Oh, okay. Well, this happened too," I said and upped my gun and shot Big Bang directly between his eyes.

"Yo, Slim! What the fuck?" Goose yelled.

"Fool me once, shame on you, but I'll be damned if you fool me twice," I said. I turned to Goose.

"Man, Slim, I did right by you. I didn't take your money," he said frantically.

"I understand that, Goose. Your mistake is that you placed your trust and my money in the hands of someone you knew was not trustworthy. I held you to a higher standard because I could tell from the moment I met you that you were an honest, down-to-earth person. I knew you and I wouldn't have any mishaps. However, you allowed someone else to cause our business to be left unfinished. So I'll tie up those loose ends," I said and then shot Goose in the forehead.

I stood over the two of them and watched them bleed out. Death had become fascinating to me. How quickly life could be lost. The shutting down of the organs and ceasing of bodily functions were especially interesting. I watched as Goose's body gave a slight twitch.

"Give me my mother fucking money, old greedy ass niggas," I said as I snatched my stacks off both of their laps. "I probably would've let you keep yours," I told Goose's dead body, "but you let your bitch ass brother get you fucked up. Thought y'all was slick. Y'all already ain't paid me and then gone take my money too. Hell, I would've let you live if this nigga wasn't your brother. I ain't got time for that revenge shit, though. Weak ass niggas! Luchesi!" I shouted. Luchesi and his crew appeared in the doorway of the office. I took one last look at Goose, Big Bang, and the big ass mess I had made, and shook my head. My adrenaline slowed and my heart rate began to steady itself, and just like that, I was over it. "Your services are required," I said and walked out of the room as they walked in and got to work.

Chapter 24

Max set up shop in Phoenix, but I wasn't into the drugs anymore. I actually wasn't into much of anything. I lounged around the house most days. I'd lay by the pool or even swim for a while. I'd go shopping on a whim and buy whatever I wanted. I'd go to steak houses and nice restaurants all by myself and turn down every drink the men sent over from the bar. I never went to any clubs, never explored the different neighborhoods. I stayed out of the way and very low key. I started going to the same hair dresser Jerri went to, the same nail salon she frequented. I didn't partake in their small talk, didn't show the least bit of interest in their gossip.

I had found the blueprints to the house, and I knew every single room inside. I knew multiple ways to get to different parts of the house, and I had even found myself a favorite little spot. Curtis had me completely in mind through every inch of the house. When I got more curious, I started exploring outside. I started test driving the different cars and sometimes I would sit in one of them and listen to the radio for hours.

I found a separate garage with ATV's, dirt bikes, and even a couple of motorcycles. I taught myself how to ride the ATV's and then the dirt bikes. When I decided to try the motorcycle, I went shopping for a suit, helmet, and boots, and assured myself that one thing was for certain: to learn to ride, I was going to have to fall. I started off slow, only riding around the perimeter of the house at a low speed. The property had more than enough room to ride as much as I wanted. I started riding off a distance from the house and coming back, and once I got comfortable with that, I started riding faster. I fell twice. Once in the beginning while I was only going about thirty miles an hour, and once while I was about eighty. I landed about a foot from hitting a tree and it knocked the window out of me, but other than being incredibly sore for weeks, I was fine.

Meanwhile, Max had been coming and going, buying and selling everything that crossed the border and making a killing from inflating his prices when he sold it across the country. He'd drop bags of money off in the bedroom he had chosen as his own little private room and he'd buy anything he wanted. He had no regular sleeping pattern. I could never expect him. We just took things as they came and loved every minute of it. We never asked each other what we were doing when we weren't around each other. We never thought too long or too hard about anything. We just lived.

So, I was out by the pool one day when my phone rang. It was Darrel. Darrel usually only called me just to check in or check on me. The only business we conducted was that Darrel would check on the house in Memphis from time to time to be sure everything was okay, and I'd throw him a few thousand for looking out for me. So I thought nothing of it when he called.

"Hello," I answered.

"Slim! Man, Slim, this shit is crazy!" The panic and excitement in his voice made me sit up on my pool chair.

"What, Darrel? What's wrong?" I asked him.

"I came over here to check on the house, right? Man, the damn police are swarming this mother fucker. So I'm clean, so I pull up and ask them what's going on. They say they got a complaint from the neighbors that there were possibly drugs in the house and some kind of drug trafficking ring going on here. Man, Slim, I fucking flipped! You and I both know there ain't shit in the damn house, but they're over here raiding the shit out of the damn house."

I just sat there taking it all in and allowed Darrel to catch his breath. I was sure he had to have been out of breath because it sounded like he said all of that in one great heaping breath. A drug complaint. It could've been worse. I was relieved. I guess I was silent a moment too long.

"Slim, did you hear me? The police are raiding your house," he repeated.

"Are you at the house right now?"

"Yeah, I'm sitting on the hood of my car in the driveway," he said.

"Okay, first of all, stop calling me Slim before they hear you. Call me Curtis if you just have to say a name, but don't say anything about me. You know all the shit I've got going on out there. Second, just let them look. They're going to search the house top to bottom. There's nothing in there, so there's nothing for you to be worried about," I told him.

"I know. It's just the point. The nearest neighbor is a mile away. Who the fuck called the police accusing you of selling drugs? Hell, who the fuck has been watching your house?"

"Now you're asking the right questions. Someone had to have been watching the house before I moved in to even notice the new movement. The thing is I didn't have much movement at all at the house, and I never loaded or unloaded anything where it could be seen from the outside. So either someone is bullshitting the police or the police are bullshitting you," I told him.

"Yeah, you're right," he said. I could tell he was looking around himself, surveying all of the police officers. "But I did see the search warrant. They are searching the house for drugs," he said.

"So the neighbors think I'm selling dope," I thought out loud.

"Looks like it."

"Well, mother fucker, I am," I laughed. "Fuck you mean."

"You a fool," Darrel laughed with me.

"Look, just play it cool," I told him. "They'll go in there and waste their time and be gone in no time."

"Aight, man. I'll call you back later."

*   ~   *   ~   *

Nothing came of the raid. They were gone within an

hour, and Darrel put the house back in order. As much of a disarray as my house in Memphis may have been in, my current home was just as out of order. The aura in the house had changed. That thing they say about a woman's intuition is not a myth. A woman knows when something is different. She can feel when something just isn't right.

I was sitting by the pool soaking in the sunrays and talking to Darrel about all of the chaos in Memphis and suddenly realized that Max hadn't been home in three days. He hadn't even called or texted me. I'm sure he knew that I was okay, but I've had male friends who I wasn't even fucking who checked on me more often than that, and this nigga was supposed to be my man. With Darrel confirming that everything was all good there, I turned my attention to what was going on around me.

I trusted Max. Everything had been the definition of copacetic between us for a long time, especially since we had been in Arizona. We both came and went as we pleased. We weren't breathing down each other's' necks or hounding each other. Of course, I wasn't doing anything wrong, so my mind wasn't focused on the possibility that Max could have been. This was unusual though. Three days? The nigga had to sleep sometimes, so where the fuck was he sleeping?

I went up to our bedroom, got out of my bikini, and laid out a gray Victoria's Secret sports bra and legging set across the bed. I turned and stared at my nakedness in the full-length mirror. I was as beautiful as I had ever been. I had picked up a few pounds that had settled themselves in all the right places. My hair had grown and had a shine to it. My skin was clear from me drinking water and it had a natural glow.

I had on no make-up; I hadn't put make-up on in weeks My own natural beauty was astonishing. I was gorgeous.

But on the inside, I felt so ugly. I had trust and jealousy issues that I had almost overcome until this moment. I had profound love for myself, and I knew that if I didn't love me no one would. No one could ever love me like I love myself, and there was no way I could claim I loved anyone else if I didn't love myself first. And that's what I did. I loved me.

I loved myself enough to be able to recognize just how much Max was destroying me on the inside. I didn't want to distrust him, but he kept giving me a reason to. The distrust was like an open wound once it cut into my insides. It festered and bled and became infected until it turned into a demon much more evil than it began as…and much more deadly.

I could feel the suspicion boiling into distrust, the distrust churning into jealousy, the jealousy bubbling over into rage. I wasn't going to continue to allow Max to do this to me. I hated the way I had begun to feel about him.

I hopped in the shower, and when I got out, I pulled my hair up into a tight slipknot, slipped into my work out clothes and tennis shoes, and then went up to Max's room. I had never gone into his room or gone through his belongings for any reason. I didn't know what to expect or even what I was looking for. I just knew I'd know when I found it.

When I opened the door, the room really didn't look too unusual. It was a smaller version of our master bedroom. It had its own bathroom and a closet that was the size of a small room. A small stack of empty black duffel bags sat in a corner. I looked around the room. There was nothing abnormal at all. I went into the closet, though, and my jaw dropped.

The shelves in the closet were built into the wall, and they were lined with stacks and stacks of money. I began opening the built-in drawers and found pounds of weed, kilos of cocaine, pills that I couldn't even identify. There was a table in the center of the closet with a small square mirror on it with cocaine residue and a straight razor on top. I was horrified at what I was seeing. Max had never done cocaine before we left Memphis. I didn't know when he had started, but it was completely unacceptable in my eyes.

There was a pile of black duffel bags in the corner. I began shuffling through them. They were filled with money, money, money. Loose ones, banded hundreds and fifties, balled up wads. I glanced slightly to my left and noticed another black bag that looked more worn than the others. I unzipped it, and it was filled with Max's clothes. It appeared to be an overnight bag Max used while he was away from home. I sorted through the clothes until I stumbled upon one little article that stopped me in my tracks.

Chapter 25

I took off running down the same trail I had been riding the motorcycle and dirt bike on. I was no health nut, but I had discovered I did my best thinking while I was running. I held my chin up and looked into the canopy of the trees as I listened to the steady pats of my feet against the ground. I had already been down this road once before with Max, and this time, it was ten times worse.

Drugs? Cocaine? I had never known Max to get high. There was telling what he was doing when he was high out of his mind. I told myself that the drugs were still not an excuse for any of his wrongdoing. There was no excusing him. I didn't even want revenge this time. I just wanted the truth. I deserved it. He dragged me into a damn relationship with him only to mistreat me. I could have been by myself and had peace of mind instead of waiting for this nigga to fulfill his promise to love me. I'd grow old waiting for that shit.

I was tired and I was fed up. I may not have found my extra hustle if it weren't for Max, but I still wouldn't have been wanting for anything. I didn't need a damn thing. My husband had made sure of that. I was hustling because I wanted to, because I had realized I was good at it. I never needed Max. I would've been just fine on my own. I would've been lonely and horny as hell, but I would've survived. Dick ain't that hard to come by.

I ran three laps around my trail to clear my mind and then jogged back up to the house. I got back into the shower, and then I went into the kitchen and started dinner. I was finishing up the steaks with onions and gravy, twice baked potatoes, shrimp, and broccoli and cheese when Max came through the door. Honestly, he looked like the biggest mess I had ever seen him look, but I treated him like he was a king coming to sit on his throne. I fixed him a drink and sat him down at the dining room table while I made his plate, the whole time notating that his eyes were blood shot red and he was fidgeting. He was high.

"Baby, are you home for the night?" I asked from the kitchen.

"For a while, but I've got to make a run later," he said.

"Damn, baby," I pouted as I came back into the dining room carrying his plate. "I thought you might have a little time to ride these curves tonight."

"You trying to surfboard tonight?" he chuckled.

"Yeah, baby. It's been a minute. I need some special attention," I said as I winked at him.

"Well, I'll see what I can do," he said as he shoved a forkful of baked potato into his mouth.

"What time do you have to leave?" I asked him as I sat down with my own plate.

"I need to head out at least by one."

"Well, it's just a few minutes after seven."

"Yeah, but I need to hop in the shower, too. I'll see how I feel, though, baby. I got you," he said.

I could tell he was lying. He didn't have the strength to have sex and he knew it. Hell, he probably hadn't been to sleep since he last left the house, and he looked like his body was ready to crash. On top of being red, his eyes were bulging slightly and his equilibrium seemed to be off. He was just a mess all around.

I purposefully ate slowly so that Max would finish before me, and when he did, I told him to leave his plate and I would take it to the kitchen. I listened as he got into the shower and then cut the TV on in the bedroom when he got out. By the time I went into the bedroom, Max was so asleep he was borderline unconscious.

I stood there and observed him as he snored. He was killing himself slowly with the drugs. I knew he probably wouldn't wake again for another twelve or more hours, so I took my time getting ready for bed. I lay down and flipped through the channels for a while, then cut the TV off, and snuggled underneath Max and fell asleep.

Waking up the next morning, I cooked a breakfast of bacon, eggs, pancakes, and sausage. I placed Max's plate and glass of orange juice on the nightstand on his side of the bed and then went back down to the kitchen to eat. I made a vegetable beef soup and a salad for lunch. I sat Max's food and canned soda on the nightstand and tossed his untouched breakfast and orange juice in the garbage. For dinner, I cooked neck bones, black eyed peas, boiled okra, and cornbread. I placed Max's plate on the nightstand again, put his empty bowl in the sink, and tossed out his untouched salad.

Max was awake and finishing his plate when I walked into the bedroom to get ready for bed. He didn't say anything. Instead, he got up, went to the bathroom, came back to bed, and went straight back to sleep. I just shook my head and laid down. Max turned over and wrapped his arms around me, but after about ten minutes he began sweating profusely and moved away from me and threw the covers off of himself.

This was ridiculous. I couldn't believe that he actually thought I was going to tolerate this bullshit. Hell, I couldn't believe that I actually had been tolerating it. Those days were over.

I followed the same routine the next morning. I got up and cooked salmon croquettes, fried green tomatoes, cheese eggs, buttered biscuits, and ham slices. I almost cooked grits, but my better judgment told me to steer clear of them before I allowed my temper to get the best of me. The smells from the kitchen must have brought back childhood memories because they awakened Max from the dead. He was awake and awaiting my entrance into the bedroom with his plate. I sat next to him on the bed and ate with him as he wolfed down the food. When I finished eating, I took both of our plates back to the kitchen.

When I came back up to the bedroom, Max was unconscious once again. I just shook my head. I hopped into the shower, threw on my gear, and took the BMW motorcycle out for a few laps. When I came back in, I made sandwiches with ham, turkey, and bacon for lunch and added a side of chips and two pickle spears- Max loved pickles- and brought him his plate again. He was still asleep, so I sat it on the nightstand knowing the poignant smell of the pickles would wake him, and the sight of a sandwich fully loaded with lettuce, tomato, cheese, mayo, and spicy mustard would be more than enough to get him up for a few minutes.

When I came back with Max's plate of meatloaf, cabbage, and mashed potatoes and gravy, he was already awake and in the shower. I knew he was getting ready to leave. He had finally slept off the drugs, though he probably still hadn't realized exactly how long he had been asleep. I just sat his plate in the same spot on the nightstand and went back to the kitchen to put the food away. I went into my closet and pulled my bike gear back out. Wrapping it inside of my long, fuzzy pink robe, I came out of the closet and headed to the bathroom while Max was sitting on the edge of the bed finishing his plate. I went into the bathroom, closed the door, and cut on the shower, letting it run while I put on my suit. Max had been fully dressed when I walked past him, so I knew he was about to head out. I'd be right behind his lying, conniving ass.

"Hey, baby?" his voice came from the other side of the bathroom door.

"Yeah?" I shouted over the running water.

"I got some runs to make. I'll be back in a few minutes," he said.

"Okay, baby," I said as I zipped up the suit and then laced up my boots. "Love you."

"I love you too, baby," he said. I waited a few moments for him to walk off and then cut the shower off. I listened as I came out of the bathroom and heard the door close downstairs. Looking at the surveillance cameras, I watched Max get into the old school low rider Chevrolet Impala he had purchased and had painted a sparkling lime green, and pull out of the gate and turn left.

I grabbed my keys and skip-stepped down the stairs to the door. I opened the bike garage, grabbed my helmet off the hook, tucked my ponytail deep into my jacket, and slipped the helmet over my head. I hopped on the bike, revved the engine, and shot down the driveway. Once I caught sight of Max's tail lights in the distance, I cut off my headlights and followed him.

I'm sick of this shit, I thought to myself as I bent the curves on the bike. I was fifteen hundred miles away from Memphis and still dealing with the same bullshit. I could've left this nigga in Memphis if I had known I was going to have to go through this shit again all the way out here. I felt stupid for having to follow this nigga to see what the fuck he had been up to just to prove to myself once again that my intuition was right. I told myself a hundred times that the shit wasn't even worth it. I tried to convince myself that I didn't need to see what I already knew to be true. But not one time did I turn around.

I follow Max into the city and into a nice neighborhood. He stopped at a gas station and got gas as I watched from across the street. Then I followed him into what looked like one of the most run-down neighborhoods in the country. That's when my heart began to race. It was all too familiar. He made a series of turns down side streets and then pulled into a driveway. I watched from down the street as he got out of the car and went inside. I pulled a pen and pad out of the breast of my suit and wrote down the address. Then I drove around to the street behind the house, parked my bike at an abandoned house, and went through the backyard to the house where Max had gone inside.

I walked around the side to a window with light inside. There were about five kids sitting on the floor gathered around an old set top TV watching "All Dogs Go to Heaven" on a VHS player. You have to be fucking kidding me, I thought to myself. I went back around the back of the house, but there were no lights on. Around the other side of the house, I peeked through another window that was dimly lit by a fifty inch flat screen perched on four crates showing "Baby Boy." There was Max, stretched out across a mattress on the floor with one flat ass pillow and a dingy sheet. A pile of empty McDonald's, Solo, and Styrofoam cups, paper plates, loose papers, and empty cigarillo wrappers was in a corner, a pile of dirty clothes in another. I was disgusted, and the whole time, this nigga looked comfortable as hell.

Then here came this nasty looking trick. She looked like an egg with legs. If Humpty Dumpty had a wife before he fell off that wall, this bitch must've been his widow. She was every bit of a hundred and eighty-five or two hundred pounds, but her thighs were the same size as her legs and looked highly incapable of supporting her weight. You know how your thighs are supposed to be wider than your legs? Well, hers weren't. I just knew her knees had to be conspiring with each other to say "fuck this shit" and run the fuck away. She had on a cheap, Walmart-looking teddy and a matching thong, both with an Aztec-looking pattern. She had a cruel idea of sexy that completely insulted the word, but she flaunted that shit like she had on my La Perla set. And Max was just lying there… looking.

She closed the bedroom door and smiled at Max. The bitch was so dark all I could really see well were her teeth. She called herself doing a little dance and popping an ass that was so flat it was damn-near inverted. Then she dropped to the floor and crawled to Max. I couldn't understand how he hadn't thrown up yet. She pulled the teddy off over her purple weave and let two of the most lifeless breasts I've even seen flop out. Then she unbuckled Max's belt and pants, pulled his completely limp dick out, and commenced to sucking it.

I could tell by her neck motions that she had no skill at all at sucking dick. I could even tell that it took her almost ten minutes of her version of sucking just to get Max's dick hard. She slid his pants and boxers off and then clumsily slipped out of her thong.

"You gone go ahead and eat it for me this time?" I heard her ask him.

"I told you I'mma do it for you one day, but not today though," he told her. "Not yet."

"Damn, mane. I just sucked the shit outta yo dick. Shit, I sucked yo shit 'til my jaws got sore. That shit is fucked up," she whined with the ugliest pout face a bitch could've possibly given him.

"Bitch, I ain't ask you for no head. Now do you want the dick or nah?" he said.

I almost busted out laughing. Bitch, you just did all that and the nigga's dick is barely medium swoll, I told her in my head. Yo ass better be happy that he even giving you some dick while you sitting there crying about some head.

"Yeah, but damn. I'm just saying," she said.

"You ain't saying shit, though, so shut the fuck up," he told her. "Damn, you done made my dick go down. Suck it and get it back hard real quick." There I was smothering my laughter again. She huffed and got up and popped his dick back in her mouth. Another seven minutes or so went by with her working furiously and when she finally came back off of it, it was almost where it was the first time. I just shook my head. This shit was a shame.

Max pulled a gold-wrapped condom from the pocket of his Robin jeans and strapped it on. She rolled over on her back like the egg she was and spread her legs. I could've cursed Max out right then. The bitch's pussy looked like some shit a nigga had chewed up and spit out.

"What the fuck you doing?" Max asked her.

"I wanna do it like this, face-to-face for a minute," she said.

"Bitch, getcho ass up and assume the damn position."

He was getting frustrated with her. She huffed again, got up, and bent over. Max rubbed his dick a few times, trying to get it just a bit harder, and then rammed it in her. She hollered out with that first thrust and never stopped. I watched

Max fuck her so hard and rough that I knew it hurt. He grabbed her by her hair and pulled it relentlessly. She turned her head and started to say something to him, but he mugged her with his other hand and pressed her face back down.

Sweating and frowning, Max pulled his dick out, took a deep breath, and then rammed his dick in her ass. I mouthed the words "oh shit" and covered my mouth with my hand. She was damn near screaming now. It was obvious she had never tried anal before. Max was fucking the shit out of her. His head leaned back and his eyes closed. It looked like he was trying to concentrate enough to bust his nut. He put both hands on her shoulders and forced his whole dick in her ass, let out a slight grunt, and just like that, it was over. Just like that, he had sealed their fate.

I got back on my bike and went home. I had work to do.

Chapter 26

Max came back home a couple of days later, but this time, I didn't dote on him. I left his ass in the bed, in the house alone most of the day to fend for himself.

When he was good and asleep, I called Luchesi, gave him the address, and hopped into Max's Impala. I pulled up in the driveway next door, hopped out of the car, and walked straight in the house with my pistol in my hand. The kids were asleep; there was no noise at all coming from their room. I crept down the hallway to the room I had figured was her room. Just as I was about to push the door open, I heard a man's voice.

"I'm finna go round here and kick it with Ty for a lil while, baby. You good?"

"Yeah, I'm straight," I heard her reply.

"Aight. Love you, boo," he told her. I ducked of into another room just as he was opening the door. He must've been about six-foot-six. He was bald and muscular, but he looked like he was about fifty years old.

I listened as he left out the front door.

"I need to call Zaddy and have him come through again," I heard her say aloud. "That dick felt good in my ass, shit," she cackled. Her nails clicked against the screen of her phone and then the phone rang on speaker until it went to the voicemail. "Damn, mane. Where he at? He always talmbout he gotta help his sister with shit," she mumbled. "He needa get from up under her cock-blocking ass and come get this pussy."

Sister? I thought to myself. Was that the lie he was telling her? Was that the excuse he was using to explain why she couldn't come over to his house? Was he telling her he lived with his sister?

"You calling my man to come back over here?" I said as I stepped around the corner.

"What the fuck? Who the fuck are you? What the fuck you doing in my house?" she said as she jumped up.

"Just know you done fucked the wrong nigga, ho," I said. I whipped out my .9 mm with its silencer already attached and shot her once in the chest. I stood over her when she fell back onto the mattress and watched her struggle to breathe. "You probably didn't even know," I told her as she lay there dying, "but just on the strength that it happened, bitch, your ass gotta get it too." I shot her once more in the forehead and called Luchesi. I checked my surroundings as I left out the door, hopped into the Impala, and went home.

I parked the car exactly where Max had left it, went into the house, fixed myself a sandwich, and then went to bed.

*   ~   *   ~   *

Max was going to be a different story, I had told myself. He wasn't going to get off nearly as easily. I wanted him to suffer.

I called Luchesi several times trying to set up an appointment, but it wasn't until about three in the evening on the second day that I received a call from a random number. It was one of his employees calling to tell me what had happened.

Luchesi and his crew had gotten to the woman's house two minutes after I called. They had been cleaning up and were almost finished and ready to throw the body in the back of their van when the six-foot-six fifty year old had suddenly returned because he left his bag of weed, and discovered Luchesi and his crew inside of the house. Luchesi being at the front of the line, he was instantly shot, and one of his employees returned fire and killed the bald giant.

"So we disposed of all three of them," the employee told me, "but we can't operate without Luchesi right now because we have to get reorganized."

"Do you have any suggestions, should I need these types of services in the future?" I asked him.

"Luchesi's biggest competition is a guy named Maurice," the man told me. "He does just as great of a job, but he's not always readily available. You'll have to set up an appointment to guarantee availability for his services most times," he explained.

He gave me Maurice's number and when I called, Maurice was happy to hear from me. I gave him the address, told him what I'd need, and then ran off to get things ready

*   ~   *   ~   *

When Max woke up that night, he had an appetite to show for how long he had slept. I fried chicken wings for him and made macaroni and cheese and green beans to go with it. When he finished, he found me in the living room watching TV.

"Slim, I gotta run somewhere for a minute," he announced. "I'll be back."

"Not so fast," I said. "Come here. I need to talk to you for a minute."

"I really need to run, Slim," he pushed the issue.

"Well, whatever it is, it's just going to have to wait because I have something I need to discuss with you," I told him. "Now, come have a seat for a second. I need to run to the bathroom real quick and then we can talk."

Max plopped down on the sofa, and I hopped up to run to the bathroom. While I was in the bathroom, my phone rang. It was the private investigator I had hired ages ago. I had forgotten all about him.

"Shonna, it's been hell trying to catch up with you," he told me. "I need to give you the information you asked me for."

"Well, can you give me a quick rundown because I'm kind of in the middle of something and I'm nowhere near Memphis right now?"

"Sure. Are you alone right now?"

"At the moment, yes."

"This guy you had me investigate- Maximillian Williams?"

"Yeah, my boyfriend."

"Your boyfriend?" he scoffed. "He's not at all who you think he is," he told me.

"What do you mean?"

"I tracked all of Maximillian's history, and was actually able to link the two of you together. Max has the same mother as you, Shonna. He was raised by your biological mother. She told him about you a few months before you two connected. He was quite upset, from what I understand, and he set out on a mission to find you. I don't know how or why he didn't convey any of this when you two connected, but he's very aware that you two are siblings," the man told me.

"Wait…Max is my brother?!" I was outraged, but still managed to control my volume.

"Yes, he is. You should probably cut ties with him immediately. He doesn't have a very extensive criminal history, but there definitely are some questionable things listed there, and this piece of information I've given you certainly makes his character questionable."

"Oh my God! Okay…okay…okay. Well, thank you for the information." I didn't even wait for a reply before I hung up.

I stood there in the bathroom mirror for a second and then took off all of my clothes. I walked through the house completely naked straight to Max. Startled by my nudity, he started to say something, but I shoved my tongue deep into his mouth. I hurriedly took off his shirt and unbuckled his belt and pants while he kicked off his shoes. He stood up and dropped his pants and boxers, revealing his rock hard dick, ready for action.

I went all in and deep throated his dick the moment it touched my lips I had him running up the couch after about two minutes, so I got off of it, bent over the back of the sofa, and Max slid straight inside of me, slow and deep.

"Max, please," I looked at him of my shoulder and said, "fuck me, baby. Fuck me hard. Make it hurt. I want it deep, hard, fast, rough."

"Yes, baby. I got you. I got you," he said. He kissed the back of my neck and then grabbed my ponytail and yanked my head back and lost control.

Max fucked me so hard it actually did hurt. The sound of our skin slapping together resounded throughout the living room. I cried out in pain that became an unbearable pleasure as he held my hips to prevent me from running.

"Take this dick, Shonna," he said through gritted teeth.

"Max!" I screamed. "Fuck me! FUCK ME!" I had never screamed so loud. I had lost all inhibitions and was deliberately yelling as loud as I could.

"Shonna, shit! Take this dick!" he growled.

"Max! Max! Max!" I screamed and then squirted juices everywhere.

Max sat down on the sofa and I immediately straddled him and slid his dick right back inside of me. I bounced hard on his dick, making sure he felt himself hitting the bottom of my pussy every single time.

Just as Max's eyes rolled back and I felt the throb in his dick, I pulled out the butcher knife I had stuck between the cushions and slit his throat with one clean slice. His hands instinctively reached for his throat.

"You trifling piece of shit," I told him. "You put me through all of this hell. Cheating on me. Beating on me. And all the while you knew you were my brother!"

He coughed as he tried to speak and choked on his own blood. His eyes were bulging in fear as he bled out.

"I'm going to fuck you until you die just to torture you even more," I told him as I bounced on him again and again. "How does it feel? This pussy good to you?" I taunted him. "I bet you loved fucking your sister's tight juicy pussy, didn't you? This is the best pussy you've ever had, ain't it? This pussy is so good to you, ain't it, Max?" I bounced hard and moaned loudly, loving every second of his death, and just as the life left his eyes, my fingers squeezed the material of the sofa, I screamed out, my walls and muscles contracted, and I came on Max's dick one last time.

234   -Slim Thick

I rose from his lap and called Maurice and then went upstairs and hopped in the shower to rinse my brother's blood off.

Epilogue

I closed the French-style mahogany double doors by their Lalique handles and then plopped back down on the sofa. My saved episodes of Family Feud began to play as my mind began to wander. I had been all over the country opening safe deposit boxes that my husband had hidden from me like they were part of a scavenger hunt. I had cars and houses most people could only dream of. But it was time for me to branch out, time for me to explore even further. It was time for me to see what my husband's off shore accounts consisted of.